The Raven Chronicles
Magic Reborn

(Book One)

Anthony D. Butler

KnightMajic Publishing—Filer, ID
ISBN: 979-8-9883348-2-8
eBook ISBN: 979-8-9883348-3-5
Library of Congress Control Number: 2023910313
Title: *The Raven Chronicles: Magic Reborn (Book One)*
Author: Anthony D. Butler
Digital distribution | 2023
Paperback | 2023

Dedication

iii

Dedicated to the memory of my father, Argie Donald Butler. He taught me to follow my dreams and made me into the person I am today. Thank you, Dad.

Chapter One

Raven stood at the edge of the Farlow cliffs surveying the canyon, waiting for her target to appear. The sun had just risen over the eastern horizon, drenching the landscape with the first light of day. A mist covered the gentle flowing Crystal River and spread out across the canyon. Raven felt the cool morning breeze brush across her face. Her long, red hair was braided behind her and her piercing green eyes watched the trail in the distance where the mist was slowly receding. She knew her target, an Elven spy, would surface here. Raven had tracked him to this location, as there was no other path up the cliff face for miles in either direction. The morning mist provided excellent cover for the elf to slip through.

Raven was no ordinary bounty hunter, however. Her tracking skills were better than anyone she had come across and, to this point, had never missed a bounty. She was so successful at bringing in her targets that those with a bounty on their heads had hunted her herself. Each time, she could turn the tables on them. For the ones who made her life especially difficult, she would just accept a lesser payment to bring them in dead rather than alive. She was ruthless in her job and had no time for nonsense like love or friendship. Being alone was her life, and she accepted it. In fact, she preferred it. No one to care for meant no one to grieve later. This way, she could live her life on her own terms and focus on her profession with no distractions.

She watched intently for signs of the elf emerging from the mist and, about an hour later, Raven saw him approach. Here she would surprise him as he emerged onto the flatland. From that point, it was a direct route to the Elven kingdom, Paelea, with no real cover until the forest several miles outside of the castle gates. She knew not to get too close as elves had superior instincts and it seemed like they could sense danger around them.

Raven had a plan to catch the elf off-guard. She had tracked his movements for a couple of weeks as he made regular trips from Paelea to Cerig, an outlier settlement that lay at the base of the Black Pine Mountains. While the land sloped gently on the north side of the canyon, the Farlow cliffs to the south were almost vertical. The trail up the cliff face had been created centuries before that included switchbacks and steep grades. Caravans would go miles to either side to avoid the treacherous climb of the narrow trail. This, she assumed, was why the elf chose this trail. Less traffic meant fewer chances to be noticed.

As swift and cunning as he was, his trek up the south side of the trail might dampen his senses. Plus, the extra time she used to track his movements might have caused him to relax a bit and think he was no longer hunted by Sacia, the human kingdom from which he was wanted. The warrant in her pouch read they sought him for the murder of an emissary, who was on his way back from Paelea on a diplomatic mission.

Raven finally spotted the elf as he appeared from the mist north of the river and monitored him as he made his way up the trail. She quietly eased back from the edge and propped herself against the rocky ledge close to where the trail emerged. She knew this was the best place to surprise him and readied her crossbow.

As Raven waited for the elf, a recurring thought crept into her mind.

This elf looks no more a spy than any I've met before, much less an assassin. He has a routine he pretty much sticks to and doesn't seem to be a loner. He seems to be well-liked by the townspeople of Cerig. I also can't believe King Rhys would order an assassination on a diplomat. He doesn't seem like that type of king.

She pushed those thoughts from her mind. It was not for her to judge a person's innocence. She was a bounty hunter. They gave her a job, and she brought them in dead or alive. If she brought them in alive, it was up to someone else to decide their fate.

She saw the elf appear, and he froze at the sound of her voice.

"Don't make any sudden moves, elf. While your warrant says to bring you in alive, it doesn't say in what condition."

"Warrant? For what?"

"Don't play dumb with me. You know damn well what."

"This is about the emissary that was murdered, isn't it?"

"You should know. You killed him."

"It wasn't me! I'm no murderer!"

"I've never heard that line before," Raven replied sarcastically.

"Yes, but I'm telling you the truth!"

"You were there, were you not?"

The elf nodded to the bounty hunter. He explained how the guards in the emissary's entourage were acting strangely when they left Paelea, so his king sent him as a scout to ensure they weren't planning some type of surprise attack on their kingdom.

"The two kingdoms signed a truce, but there are those in Sacia who are not happy with it. The guards must have suspected they were being followed."

"They probably figured it out once you attacked the emissary."

"I swear to you I didn't even go near the emissary!"

"Your words mean nothing to me, elf. I have heard every excuse, and yours is no different."

"Tell me, bounty hunter, do you sleep well at night knowing you might take someone to their death who is innocent?"

"Proving innocence or guilt is not my concern. I accept contracts to bring in fugitives on the run. A trial will decide your fate."

"You know trials can be bought. There are those within the walls of Sacia that want war resumed with the elves. They want our lands and our wealth."

"King Warrick is an honorable man. I am certain he will ensure the trial is fair and just."

"You are naïve to believe that."

"Again, not my concern. Now throw this collar on and tie this rope to it. If you try to escape, you will regret it."

Raven laid her crossbow down and walked up to the elf to check his knot. As she observed the collar and pulled out another rope for his hands, the elf struck Raven and knocked her back. He hurried toward the crossbow but felt himself jerk hard backwards and slammed to the ground. Raven walked over to him, holding the rope to his collar in her hands.

"Nice try, elf. I figured you would try something stupid like that, though I'm surprised you landed as hard of a punch as you did. Now get up!"

Raven pulled him up by the rope and he staggered forward a bit, his head pounding from hitting the ground.

"Consider that a warning. Next time you pull something stupid like that, I will break a knee… or both."

Raven tied his hands and mounted her horse, Shadow, and ordered the elf to walk ahead. She rested her crossbow in her lap as they started their journey to Sacia.

Chapter Two

The Sacian guards watched Raven approach the large gray castle that sat on top of a broad hill overlooking the surrounding land. She surveyed the battle-worn walls surrounding the castle and was thankful for the truce between the two kingdoms. She had known only about war in her lifetime. It had started before the two current kings came to power. The previous Elven king was the first to pass away. His heart gave out from old age. In his last few weeks, his advisors fought the war as he lay in bed, dying. The human king was killed in battle around the same time as he tried to save a regiment of his men trapped behind enemy lines. The king had taken a dozen of his best warriors in a surprise attack but were overwhelmed as the elves had reinforcements nearby. They knew the king's bold reputation and suspected he would try to free his men. Many thought this might be the end of the war, but decades-long hostilities prevented any type of ceasefire. King Warrick of Sacia was the first attempt to end the war. Both kings agreed that war between the kingdoms must end as the hatred their fathers had toward each other died with them. They also knew their people were tired of war, but hard feelings still existed between the two kingdoms. That would take a long time to mend, but Warrick and Rhys knew they had to try. The ceasefire gave them a chance to rebuild their villages while an official treaty was being drawn up by King Warrick. He would then submit it to King Rhys for his input. Hopefully, the two sides could come to an agreement that would benefit both sides. Villages and farmland had become battlefields and food supplies were low. The Elven people were more resourceful, but they were also beginning to feel the effects of their war-torn lands. They were grateful for the truce, but Sacia was divided, especially among the nobles. Many thought their new king was weak for being the first to reach out to their enemy.

Raven understood Sacia was teetering on a civil war. She hoped she could deliver the prisoner and leave with her payment without incident. As she approached the gates, she waved at the guards while Shadow trotted into the courtyard with the elf in front. A couple of guards within the courtyard approached her and stared for a moment at the elf and then turned their attention to Raven. They told her they would take the prisoner and she could see Lord Cameron regarding payment.

Raven shook her head. "I am under strict orders by King Warrick to deliver this prisoner to him personally."

"The king is busy at the moment and asked us to hold the prisoner until he becomes available."

"Then I will wait until he's no longer busy."

Raven pulled a scroll from a pouch tied around her waist. "This scroll states that under no circumstances am I to leave the prisoner with anyone except him. Unless you have a scroll that states otherwise, you will move aside and allow me to take my horse to the stables. My guest and I can wait in the tavern until I receive word that the king is ready to see me."

The guards looked at each other and grumbled, but they waved Raven on. They glared at her until she was out of sight. A third guard nodded at the other two and followed behind them. Raven glanced back and noted the third guard following them. She also noticed his hand on the hilt of his sword. Raven looked at the elf and then back at the guard. She knew tensions were high, but this just seemed over the top. The elf looked back at her with a worried look.

"They mean to separate us. If they can get me away from you and out of sight, they will kill me. They do not want me delivered to the king."

"Well, what they want and get are two different things. Either you are delivered directly to King Warrick, or we leave here together. I would rather make enemies of the ones scheming against the king than to make an enemy of the king himself."

Raven secured Shadow in the stables and dropped a gold coin in the stable boy's hand with an unspoken understanding to care for her horse. The boy's eyes lit up and nodded at Raven and she returned a smile. She then escorted the elf to the tavern. As they were about to enter, the two original guards approached, along with someone dressed a bit more formally. "We just received word that the king is now available, and we shall take you to him."

"Really? That quick, huh?"

"Word got to him that the prisoner was here, so he cut his meeting short."

"How convenient."

"Do you dare call us liars, bounty hunter?"

"Not at all. Just lucky for me is all. I thought I was going to have a long wait ahead of me."

"Sir Turstan here will escort you both up to the king's chambers."

Raven felt a sudden burning sensation run through her, but she kept her composure. "Thank you" is all she said and nodded to Sir Turstan to lead her to King Warrick. Two different guards approached as they neared the castle door. Raven realized what might be happening.

"There's no need for you two to tag along. This elf's not going anywhere." She looked at the elf. "We came to an understanding."

"Sorry miss, king's orders. We will join you, just in case."

"Well, if the king insists, who am I to argue? Come on elf. The king awaits."

The elf whispered back. "I wouldn't count on it."

Raven rolled her eyes and nudged him in front of her as the guards led them into the castle. Through the main entrance, a cavernous room with marble floors and colorful tapestries greeted them. Along the walls, paintings hung with golden frames of previous kings, queens, and famous nobility. King Warrick's painting hung in the center of all as the reigning king. The room's ceiling easily rose at least two levels and was quite breathtaking. She noticed the elf had temporarily forgotten his fate and admired the artistic look at the entrance.

"A little different from Paelea, huh?"

The elf shook out of his awe to look back at Raven. "It's beautiful, but a little extravagant. Paelea tries to give a more modest appearance."

"Agreed. It's a bit much for my taste, but it is insightful to see how others live, is it not?"

"I've always dreamed of traveling past these lands to see new and interesting places, but now, I know I will never see them, as I fear I will never leave this palace."

One guard overheard their conversation. "You've got that right, elf. You have a visit with the gallows soon!"

Raven arched an eyebrow at the guard. "You are already

convinced he's guilty."

"Of course, he's guilty. He's an elf and was spotted where the emissary was murdered."

"Well, I think there might be more to it, and I am sure King Warrick will uncover the truth."

"Yeah, sure bounty hunter. If that makes you feel better."

The guards laughed to themselves and led the two further into the castle. As they wound up a circular set of stairs, Raven noticed their path differed from the usual one.

"I thought King Warrick's chamber was in a different part of the castle?"

"That's his main chamber. Where we're going is more private. He wished not to be disturbed when he meets with you."

"Ah, I see. Makes sense."

Raven watched the elf. He was looking around nervously, and she could see he was fidgeting with his hands. None of this made any sense. Assassins weren't this scared when caught. Most even poisoned themselves so as not to be interrogated. Her doubts toward the guards' motives grew. The feeling she had earlier, the one that always seemed to warn of impending danger, was back at a fever pitch. She held it down and kept her stoic appearance. She knew the guards were not taking her to the king, but she was curious about where they were going.

Suddenly, three guards appeared behind them. Raven glanced back and measured them.

"All this for a single elf? It's a bit much, don't you think?"

"The king knows others here might take matters into their own hands, so he wanted to make sure no one else got to him first."

"Understood." Raven turned her attention to the elf, who was staring at her now. "Something you want to say, elf?"

He just shook his head, and the guard directly behind him gave the elf a shove. Raven quietly removed one of three small daggers she kept hidden in her belt and bumped the elf's hand and slipped him the weapon. The elf grabbed it and fought the urge to look back at Raven. He was confused, but relieved that he might have an ally with the bounty hunter. He kept his head forward so as not to attract any further attention.

At the top of the stairs and through the door, a hallway stretched through the upper portion of the castle. No tapestries or any other decorations were to be found, which told Raven this area was off-limits to visitors. Several hundred feet ahead, the guards stopped at a large wooden door to the left, knocked, and waited for the door to open. They led Raven and the elf into a spacious room with a single tall but thin window and a desk in the middle.

They led both to the table, and a door opened from the right side of the room, but it was not the king that stepped through.

"Lord Cameron, what is the meaning of this?" Raven demanded. "I am to see King Warrick directly." Raven noticed four more guards along with the guards present with them. Nine against two. Ten, if you counted Cameron. She did not like these odds. The elf shot her an 'I told you so' look. Raven glared back at him.

"Ahh, Raven. So good to see you again, as always. My apologies as the king is tied up with another important meeting and cannot be disturbed. I assure you I am aware of your deal with him, and he wants the prisoner handed over to me. I have your payment here for you."

Cameron tossed a coin purse onto the table. "Just leave the elf with me and you may go."

Raven shook her head. "I am not releasing him to you. The elf and I will return to the tavern and will wait for the king to see me. Come find me when he's not... busy." Raven turned to leave, but the guards stepped in front of the door to block her exit. Raven turned and shot Cameron an icy glare.

Cameron sat down at the desk and looked at the elf, and then turned his attention to Raven. After a moment, he leaned toward her. "I don't think you understand, bounty hunter. You will release this elf to me by order of King Warrick or else you will be arrested."

Raven laughed. "Arrested? I have it here in the scroll that I am to deliver him to the king and under NO circumstances am I to do otherwise."

Cameron simply smiled at Raven and leaned back in his chair. "No, I think you will release him to me. Did you really think the king would ever see this elf alive? Look around Raven. You are outnumbered and these are elite guards behind me. Had you just handed him over, you could have walked out of here a wealthier woman, but now you won't walk out of here at all. Guards! Kill them!"

Raven quickly looked at the elf and in a quick swipe, slashed through the rope that bound his hands with a dagger she had snuck out during the back and forth with Cameron. "I hope for our sakes you can fight elf!"

The elf nodded and ducked as a sword came about his head. Raven turned and threw the dagger at one guard, and it landed right in his eye socket. The guard screamed, and Raven turned her attention to the next one. The elf made his way to the edge of the room to draw some attackers away from Raven. As two guards moved to attack him, he dodged their swords with ease and sliced one of the knight's wrists, causing him to drop his sword. The elf caught it in mid-air and turned around and landed a blow to the back of the other knight as he readied his sword for another attack. Cameron, seeing the commotion in front of him, grabbed the coin purse off the table and quietly slipped from the room through the door he came in. He glanced over his shoulder and watched for a moment before ducking out. Raven had taken some serious cuts but had drawn her sword and was holding her own. She had already disposed of the two guards and was now engaging four others. The elf used his quickness to overwhelm his attackers. He made his way to the door, opened it, and yelled for Raven to follow. She swung her sword at the remaining guards, turned and ran down the hall, following the elf. They could hear shouting behind them, but they made it to the stairs and started running down as fast as they could. They were much quicker than the armored guards and reached the bottom and burst into the main area and raced to the doors. Before the guards nearby knew what was happening, the elf and the bounty hunter were already out of the castle and headed toward the stables. Raven didn't have time to saddle her horse, so she just reached for the elf's hand and pulled him up behind her. "Hold on!"

"How are we going to get through the gate?"

"By force if we have to!" Raven yelled back.

Shadow, on her own, took off galloping as soon as they were seated, sensing urgency from Raven. They rushed out of the stables and toward the gate. The guards looked confused and didn't know what was going on. That gave Raven the moment she needed. She nudged Shadow to go faster, and the horse obliged. By the time the guards chasing them reached the courtyard, Raven and the elf were already at the gate. The guards yelled in vain for the gate to be closed, but by the time they heard the order, the bounty hunter and the elf were free beyond the wall. The horse continued galloping until they reached the forest at the bottom of the hill and then slowed to a trot. Raven looked behind her to make sure they weren't close to them, but just in case, she guided Shadow off the main trail and through the woods, away from any would-be chasers.

Raven and the elf rode in silence until the elf spoke up.

"By the way, my name is Erinoth."

She nodded at him. "I know."

"You know? Then why call me elf if you knew my name?"

"It helps in my line of work not to get close to my prisoners."

"Is that what I still am? A prisoner?"

"Yes… no, maybe. I don't know, to be honest. Give me some time to think it over. Don't try to escape either. My mood is not one to trifle with right now."

"I won't. I'm just glad we made it out of there alive."

"Yeah, me too."

Erinoth noticed Raven's blood-soaked shirt. "Are you okay?"

Raven looked down at her shirt and just shrugged. "I've been in worse shape."

"Worse than this? Have you ever considered a new line of work, then?"

Raven wiped her brow with her sleeve and sighed. For a moment, she said nothing, as if lost in thought. She then turned her head back to him and finally answered.

"After this, I probably won't have a choice."

Chapter Three

King Warrick finished his daily meeting with his advisors and decided since it was such a beautiful day, he would take a walk along the castle wall and observe the day's activity. Tall, with broad shoulders, his frame epitomized royalty. Long, brown hair, touched with a little gray on the sides, spilled out from under his crown and onto his shoulders. His dark blue robe flowed behind him in the warm breeze of the afternoon. Escorted by a couple of his finest knights, he walked slowly, taking in all the bustling on the grounds below. From traders busy selling their wares to kids playing in the courtyard, Warrick's leathered face smiled at the peaceful scene below. Not a cloud dotted the skies above, which was not uncommon this time of year. When it did rain, it left the streets looking like rivers but kept the crops alive. People who noticed him would stop and give a quick bow and he would wave back, but most just went about their business.

Warrick wasn't the type of king that demanded everyone bow before him. He thought of himself as the people's king, and he saw the crown only as a necessary evil to keep order in the kingdom. Warrick wanted nothing more than to have peace so that people could move about as they wished and prosper. He knew that by being kind to the populace, there would be fewer problems to deal with. Still, he felt a sense that something wasn't right within the halls of his own castle. He would pass by random guards speaking until he came near, and they would immediately hush. Warrick would politely ask what they were speaking of, and they would simply reply the usual: ladies, ale or gambling of some sort.

Warrick knew the truce between Sacia and Paelea was not very popular among the royals, specifically those loyal to his brother-in-law, Lord Cameron. They had always disagreed on how to handle relations with the Elven people. Cameron viewed them as a lower species to humans. He wanted the Elven people conquered with only a few nobles spared the guillotine for use as servants. It infuriated him when Warrick had proposed the truce. Warrick claimed whatever hatred existed between the two kingdoms was because of old grudges that no longer existed. Decades before, what appeared to be a misunderstanding between the two kings escalated into an all-out war. Both kings were too proud to admit that either might be wrong. Because of their foolishness, both armies had completely ravaged the land to where both kingdoms were struggling to even feed their own soldiers, much less their citizens. Warrick, as well as King Rhys of Paelea, knew if they did not end this senseless war that both kingdoms would be ripe for invasions from the far lands. He could not make Cameron understand this because of the lord's blind hatred for the Elves. Warrick remembered a time when his brother-in-law didn't carry the hatred he did now. Warrick's wife, Renee, was out with her ladies one day when they came across an Elven warrior who was lying on the edge of a creek, wounded, and dying from a battle the previous day. Renee tried to help the warrior the best she could, but he died shortly after. An Elven hunting party then came upon them and tried to capture her and her entourage, but Renee resisted and slipped from her captor's grip. As she stumbled backward, she fell and hit her head on a boulder by the stream, killing her instantly. As the women who had come with her screamed, the hunting party panicked and vanished through the woods.

Heartbroken by the news, Warrick understood it was an accident and that the elves would never kill a non-soldier in cold blood. The queen's maidens had said as much. However, Lord Cameron would not be as forgiving. His disdain for the Elven people morphed into pure hatred upon hearing of his sister's death. His relationship with Warrick soured as well, and with the news of the truce, Warrick knew he might have problems with Cameron. He did not want to imprison his brother-in-law since he was still family to him. Not to mention his son Liam and Cameron had a close relationship. Now, though, Warrick feared Cameron might plan some sort of coup to remove him from power.

Two figures running from the castle snapped his mind back to the present. He recognized the woman as the bounty hunter Raven. The other was an elf. They appeared to be running from someone. He watched intently as they both ran to the stables and returned with the elf riding with her. He then saw who they were running from: his own guards. Even from where he was, he could almost feel their hatred. They yelled for the gate to be closed, but Raven and the elf were gone by the time they realized what was happening. Warrick became angered at the scene. While he knew little about the bounty hunter, he knew she was trustworthy. She was supposed to bring the prisoner directly to him, but for reasons unknown, Raven fled with the elf from his soldiers. She had brought the prisoner to the castle, but something caused them to leave in a rush. It took little for him to guess who might be behind this. He turned to his knights and motioned for one to hurry down and demand the men who chased Raven to stay where they were. He told the others to follow him down to the courtyard.

The king's knight reached the courtyard as several guards had mounted their horses, ready to go after the bounty hunter and elf. He demanded the guards at the gate to prevent their departure. The guards on horseback sneered at him.

"How dare you halt our chase of the two prisoners! On what authority do you have?"

"Mine!" King Warrick approached angrily.

They immediately bowed their heads to the king. "Your Majesty! The prisoners are escaping!"

"For one, the bounty hunter is NOT a prisoner! Second, the elf is a suspect, not convicted. I only wanted him here for questioning. Do either of you want to explain why they felt terrified to speak to me?"

"She wouldn't release the elf, sir."

"Was I present?"

"N-No sir."

"She was under a direct order only to release the elf TO ME!"

Lord Cameron came out to meet the king. He gave the guards a quick look and then turned to King Warrick and bowed.

"Please forgive them, your highness. It is a misunderstanding on my part. I was unbelieving that the bounty hunter was serious when she said to deliver them only to you. She gave no proof and as a bounty hunter, it is hard to take one at their word. I thought she was simply being stubborn."

Warrick, still upset over the events he witnessed, dismissed the guards, but then turned to Cameron.

"I know your hatred of elves is blinding, but if I find out that you had other plans for the elf behind my back, you will lose my favor and no one in this kingdom can save you. Is that understood?”

“Perfectly, your Majesty. I swear I was only going to hold them until you were freed up and then I was going to alert you to his presence. The bounty hunter became paranoid for no reason and attacked us, fled, and now they are free beyond the castle.”

“I will deal with the bounty hunter myself. You may leave now, but I had better not hear of something like this happening again, understood?”

Cameron nodded and turned back to the castle. Warrick watched him leave and thought to himself that something was amiss in his castle. He was sure of it now. He could tell his brother-in-law was lying. The only question was how many of his trusted advisors felt as Cameron did? Was he safe with his own guards? Warrick knew he had to root out this treachery before they could carry out any coup, and he felt he had little time to find out.

Chapter Four

Raven and Erinoth traveled slowly and quietly through the forest. She did not want to push Shadow too hard in case they needed to make another quick escape. Raven guided Shadow to a nearby stream to rest. The two unexpected companions remained mostly silent for the longest time until Raven finally spoke.

"You realize my days as a bounty hunter are over, thanks to you."

"I am sorry, Raven. I tried to warn you they would try to kill me."

"Indeed, you did. I did not expect them to try to kill me, however."

"They would have let you go had you simply handed me over to them."

"I could not go against the king's wishes, no matter what happened."

"So, it had nothing to do with me being innocent?"

"I told you before, I don't care if you're innocent or guilty. I am not a judge or a king."

"You have a gift though, do you not? You knew deep down I did not kill that emissary."

Raven tightened her lips but acted as if she did not hear him.

"I will make sure you return safely to Paelea, but then I need to leave and figure out how I can contact King Warrick. He must be told of Lord Cameron's treachery."

"I will be fine to make my way back to Paelea from here, granted I don't run into any more bounty hunters."

"I had a helluva time tracking you down, Erinoth, and it may sound arrogant, but I am the best bounty hunter there is."

"Perhaps because there is more to you than you know. Druids and sorcerers have these same… senses as you. Usually, a power such as this is passed down through generations. Maybe your parents…"

Raven cut him a look and Erinoth knew immediately he had crossed a line he shouldn't have. He quietly apologized and went over to sit down beside a tree away from Raven. Raven watched him for a moment and then turned to Shadow.

"Girl, what have we gotten ourselves into? I can deal with the occasional thug and his henchmen, but knowing an entire kingdom may hunt me down may be too much to deal with. If I can't figure this out soon, I may find a new home beyond the Black Pine Mountains."

Once Raven felt Shadow had rested enough, she told Erinoth it was time to move on so they could reach the forest's edge by nightfall. Something had been nagging at her since they arrived at the creek, but she kept it to herself so as not to evoke more discussion on the matter. She knew she could not have left the elf in the hands of Lord Cameron, as he would be dead by now. However, this talk of her being more than just a bounty hunter was just nonsense.

As they left the creek, a figure appeared in front of them. Dressed in a purple hooded robe, the person held up their hand for them to stop. This had been what Raven was sensing but could not figure out until now.

"Are you in trouble?" Raven asked after several moments of silence. The person lowered their hood to reveal a young female with long, black hair and piercing blue eyes. She looked at them both, but turned and gave Raven an almost sinister grin.

"No, but I think you are."

Chapter Five

King Rhys, the Elven king, agreed with King Warrick on his views of the previous war. He felt the two kingdoms could be allies but knew it would probably take years to mend hurt feelings. He accepted the truce and hoped in time they could come to an agreement on a permanent treaty. There were still some borderland disputes between the two kingdoms, but Rhys believed they could solve this with diplomacy instead of blood. However, in this period of fragile peace, he felt he needed to ensure the emissary visit wasn't a ruse for something more. He wanted to believe the rumors that King Warrick was an honest man, but a prolonged war made him a little wary to trust anyone at this point.

He called for his aide, Aeson, and asked if anyone had heard from Erinoth. He had not come back from his usual trip to Cerig. It was unlike him to be so late. Aeson responded no one had mentioned him returning. Rhys creased his brow and told his aide if he hadn't heard from his scout by morning, he was to send out a search party.

Rhys turned around to see his daughter, Princess Amedee, approaching. He was so lost in thought that he hadn't seen her walk in. The look on her face was concerning.

"What's wrong, Amedee?" Rhys asked.

"I overheard Aeson asking a couple of guards if Erinoth had returned."

"No. It is unlike him not to report to me. I hope that perhaps he was simply delayed."

"You don't think the Sacians captured him, do you?"

Rhys's face turned grim. "Even if they did, I would expect word to come from Sacia, explaining why. While King Warrick appears to be a man of honor, there is no doubt some in Sacia want war to continue. What Warrick has done is brave, but it might also be very dangerous for him and anyone close to him."

"Why would they still want war? Their land is as war-torn as ours. They must see this."

"Men with evil in their hearts do not listen to reason. They want blood, but they also want our land. We are a wealthy kingdom, and some want that wealth all to themselves. However, I will not just sit by quietly. If something has happened to Erinoth, I will have to consider every option. I know our soldiers are weary and need an extended rest, but they must understand their homes are still at risk and they may still be called upon. I will give Erinoth more time, but if he has not returned by morning, we will conduct a search party. If we find Sacia is involved with his disappearance, there will be a reckoning, and the truce will end."

"Father, if I must, I will raise a sword to fight for Paelea. I have trained almost my whole life for this."

King Rhys chuckled at his daughter.

"Do you mock me, father?"

"Quite the opposite. I know your skill and bravery match any of our warriors, which is why I would need you here. Should war find us once again, I need you here not for your safety, but to lead the army within these walls should an attack fall on the castle while I am away. I have every bit of faith in you, Amedee. Now, enough of this talk of war. I am sure there is a reasonable explanation as to why he has not returned, and I intend to find it."

Amedee, satisfied with her father's explanation, said nothing else but bowed and exited. Rhys watched her go and his face turned grim. He hated not knowing what might happen, and he hated worrying his daughter even more. The longer Erinoth's absence stretched out, he knew there would be calls for a retaliation, no matter how much he pleaded with the Elven people. They protected their own and there was already a built-up distrust of humans from the war. He was not completely sure if the truce could last. Thankfully, he had the trust of his people, but even that would only go so far.

Rhys looked out his window toward Sacia. "Erinoth, I pray for your safe return to us and soon. This kingdom can't survive another war."

Chapter Six

Prince Liam stood at the edge of the lake and soaked in the peacefulness that surrounded him. A light, cool breeze blew in from the north and he watched a hawk dive to the water and climb back to the sky, holding a fish in his talons. *Such is the cycle of life*, Liam thought. For decades, he watched as humans and elves struggled to be the hawk. While success and failure existed on both sides, the war had seen no clear victory, and both kingdoms suffered for it, and its citizens suffered the most from it. Well, most of the human kingdom was tired of war. Liam shook his head at the faction that had wanted the war to continue. They felt as if they were finally gaining the upper hand on the Elven people and wanted one last battle to crush them. Had the previous king not fallen ill and died, they might have succeeded. However, King Warrick bore no hatred for the elves, nor did he have any desire to destroy their lands for what he deemed a greedy lust for riches.

Liam closed his eyes and soaked in his surroundings but failed to hear the footsteps behind him. By the time he heard the sword being unsheathed, he could only get his hand down to the hilt of his own sword before he felt the pressure on his back. He raised his hands in the air and asked what the intruder wanted.

"All I want is your head, prince."

Liam grinned. "Well, if you want it, you will have to kill me for it." Liam took a step forward, pulled his sword and spun around to face his bodyguard, Evan.

Evan blocked Liam effortlessly. "So, it shall be."

Both men attacked and defended with the experience of battle-hardened soldiers. Only once when Liam wildly swung at his bodyguard, did Evan parry Liam's move and thrust with one of his own, slicing Liam on the upper arm.

Liam stumbled back and glanced down at the tear in his shirt. "I just had this tailored. You shall pay for this!"

"Perhaps you should not fight as a child would."

Liam pounced and parried another attack and, with his foot, swiped at Evan's leg and knocked him off-balance. By the time Liam advanced to strike a blow of his own, Evan quickly recovered and knocked at Liam so hard that Liam's knees buckled and then another quick thrust jarred Liam's sword from his hand. Evan advanced and rested his sword on Liam's chest. "Give?"

Liam nodded, raising his hands. "I give."

Evan sheathed his sword and reached out with his hand to help his friend to his feet. Instead, Liam grabbed Evan's arm and flipped him over, and his bodyguard landed on his back with a thud.

"So, this is how you treat the person who just spared your life?"

Liam laughed. "Sorry, I had to soften the humiliation of losing to you."

Even stood up and brushed himself off. "You always lose to me. That's why I'm your bodyguard. You need me to protect you."

"Please. I can take care of myself. I let you be my bodyguard, so you'd quit asking me for money. Now I just pay you to follow me around."

"And yet you always sneak away, and I must hunt you down. At least now I know all your hiding spots. I just need to figure out which one you disappear to."

"Looks like it's time to find new spots, then."

"Indeed." Evan then gave his friend a troubled look.

Liam's smile disappeared. "Something on your mind?"

"We just had an incident at the castle. The bounty hunter Raven brought in an elf suspected of the murder of Emissary Godwin.

"That's good," Liam noted. "She always seems to come through for my father."

"Yes, except she was then seen running from the guards with the elf in tow and escaped from the castle."

"What? There must be some mistake."

"Your father stopped the guards from chasing after them. He knows if Raven left without seeing him first, then something spooked her. He thinks someone interfered."

"Let me guess, Lord Cameron."

"That's who he suspects."

"It's no secret he was against my father's truce, but I don't think he would betray him. My father allowed him to keep his title after my mother died. He could have stripped my uncle of everything."

"Agreed, but something happened for Raven to abandon her duty."

Liam thought for a minute. "Let's go see my father. Perhaps we could help him in this matter."

"My thoughts exactly."

Liam patted his friend on the back, and both headed back, concerned about what lay ahead.

Chapter Seven

Raven watched the young woman for a moment. "What do you mean, we're in trouble? You don't even know us."

"Not him, only you. You do not know who you are, but I do. She also knows you and will come for us both soon."

"You do not know who I am. Who are you and who is this she you speak of?"

"Raven, I know exactly who you are."

Taken aback, Raven became aggravated toward the strange woman. She unsheathed her sword and pointed it toward the woman. "How do you know my name?"

The woman just shrugged. "Just know we are alike, but you are stubborn and will refuse to accept it."

Raven glared at Erinoth, daring him to say anything. "I know who I am, and it's nothing like you. If you are finished with your games, we really need to be on our way."

"Worry not about Sacia. There is darkness coming. Something more sinister than two kingdoms squabbling over trinkets. If you are to survive this, you will need to learn who you truly are."

Raven's anger boiled to the service. "Stop with this nonsense! There is no darkness, and I am in no mood for riddles!"

Raven motioned for Erinoth to leave when the woman's smile widened, and she nonchalantly twisted her hand. Raven and Erinoth stood frozen in place.

"Understand this, bounty hunter. You can leave when I allow it. You may think I'm crazy, but I have seen the future through a vision. This is not some handed down prophecy coming to fruition. This is an evil that will destroy this land. She seeks revenge, though I do not know why. You can deny your birthright, but when you finally see and understand, it may be too late for us all. I cannot defeat her alone."

"Defeat who? You still haven't said who you or this other person is."

"My name is unimportant, and the woman hasn't revealed who she is yet." The woman's eyes started glowing a purplish hue. She released them from their paralysis and turned her hands out, and a purple mist appeared in them. "Beware the danger coming. Erinoth, warn your king. He needs to understand that war with Sacia is pointless. She will destroy Sacia but won't care if Paelea is caught in the crossfire." The mist expanded to cover her entire body, and then the strange woman vanished.

Erinoth stared at where the woman stood just moments before.

"I heard a sorceress existed in this forest, but I thought it was simply a legend."

"Apparently not. She's been hiding out here for so long that she's gone mad. Be thankful she did not want to harm us. Let's be on our way."

"But Raven, she knew us… by name. She knows of my king."

"Okay, fine. She knows us. This just means we should get away from here as quickly as possible."

"You don't think we should take her warning seriously?"

"What? About some darkness coming? Come on Erinoth. She's just a crazy witch trying to mess with our minds. It's probably how she breaks up the boredom of hiding. Let's get you back to Paelea and forget this ever happened."

Erinoth pleaded with Raven to at least consider the possibility, but she refused to discuss the matter further. She gave an icy demeanor toward her companion, but her mind refused to dismiss the words the woman had spoken. For her to be a hermit and isolated in the forest, she seemed to know about the two of them. This bothered Raven. She would have to figure this out later, but her immediate concern was escorting Erinoth back to Paelea. It appeared that Sacia was closer to civil war than she first thought, and she wedged herself right in the middle of it. She wondered if her days as a bounty hunter were indeed over.

Chapter Eight

Several miles from the border of Paelea, Raven stopped just before they topped a grassy hill. The sun had already set, and they were still several hours from the edge of the forest that spanned to the castle. She hoped to reach the cover of the forest before dawn, but she sensed potential trouble ahead. Before, she would have just passed it off as a good instinct. Now she caught herself questioning it in her mind. She continued her coldness toward the elf. She had to. One crack and she wouldn't be able to shut him up about their encounter with the mysterious witch.

Raven motioned Erinoth off Shadow. She quietly dismounted and snuck up to the top of the hill. While night was taking hold of the land, a waxing moon shone from above and in the twilight, Raven noticed silhouettes of men on horseback dotting the landscape. She cursed under her breath. While they stopped for rest, Sacian soldiers had ridden on and set up a trap just below the border. There was no way this could be by the order of King Warrick. This had to be Lord Cameron going behind the king's back. This was a bold move by him. If Warrick found out, he would be tried for treason. Cameron had to have an endgame. No time to worry about that right now with her current situation. She could tell there were too many to fight head-on, and she wondered how spread out they were. She eased back to where Erinoth and Shadow were and whispered what she found. Erinoth motioned for them to backtrack some and head for a more easterly direction than their northern track. She nodded as she understood where he was leading them. While the detour was further, they would venture into some thicker brush that might hide them long enough to make a break for the border. She knew this would be hard on her horse, but she felt if they could cover enough ground and put enough distance between themselves and the soldiers, she could ease up on Shadow. Once they reached the border, hopefully they would find a Paelean patrol nearby.

Raven and Erinoth eased their way through the thicket, sustaining cuts from the thorny bushes they had to maneuver through. Once they approached the clearing, they could no longer see the soldiers, and they hoped the same was true for them. Raven checked Shadow and found she had made it through okay cuts and all. Raven and Erinoth eased onto Shadow and with one kick of her heel, Shadow took off at a full gallop. Her hoofs beat along the ground as she darted for the border that lay a few miles ahead. Raven didn't turn to see if the soldiers had seen them, but Erinoth looked back and saw a rider off to their left coming fast toward them. They were spotted and now the race was on. Shadow sprinted ahead and slowly gained distance from the soldiers, who were slowed by their heavy armor. Up ahead was the border, but she knew the army was desperate to catch them as too much was at stake if they failed.

Raven peered ahead and suddenly pulled back on the reins. She jerked Shadow to the right as more soldiers appeared in the distance.

"They're persistent, I'll give them that!" Raven swore to herself as she looked for somewhere to go. A barrage of arrows landed close by and Erinoth pointed toward where the archers were. They were so close. If they could just make it to the border. Raven suddenly heard a commotion ahead. They watched in confusion as the archers hurriedly retreated south.

"What the-" Before Raven could finish her sentence, Erinoth pointed toward the north.

"Head there! They're Paelean!"

"Are you sure?" Raven questioned. "If not, this will be the end of us."

"I'm sure! They must have been nearby and heard the commotion."

"Or looking for you. Either way, Shadow needs to rest. Come on, girl, give me just a little more!"

Raven steered Shadow toward the oncoming party and slowed down as the Paelean commander broke from the group and approached them. Immediately, he recognized Erinoth and turned to glare at Raven.

"Who are you?"

"I'm Raven."

"The bounty hunter?"

"Yes."

The commander looked over at Erinoth.

"Are you alright? King Rhys has been concerned about your extended absence."

"About that. I need to see King Rhys at once."

"And what of this bounty hunter? Should we detain her?"

Erinoth looked over at Raven and gave a mischievous grin. Raven rolled her eyes.

"No, commander. She needs to speak to the king as well. A situation has developed that needs his attention."

The commander nodded but pointed to the south.

"Who were those men chasing you? Were they from Sacia?"

"Well, yes, and no."

"Explain."

"That is why we need to speak to the king. It's, well, complicated."

"So it seems. Very well. Bounty hunter, follow us and we will have a detail form in the rear."

"Understood commander."

"I must also ask that you surrender your weapons to us. We will return them once this matter is cleared up."

Raven hesitated for a moment, but then nodded to the commander. She handed over her crossbow, sword, daggers, and a shiv she had hidden in her boot.

"Erinoth has another of my daggers, but he can keep it. It seemed to bring him a little luck."

The Elven commander nodded.

"If that's everything, let's move. I'm not ready to restart a war with Sacia just yet."

*****

King Rhys was on the upper level of the castle, just outside his private chamber. He was speaking with a guard when Aeson approached. Rhys dismissed the guard and turned his attention to his most trusted aide, who promptly bowed.

"Any news of Erinoth?"

"Yes, your Majesty. He has returned."

"He has? Where is he?"

"He is in the dining hall. He's had quite the ordeal, apparently."

Rhys gave his aide a concerned look. "I assume there is more to this."

"The bounty hunter Raven is with him."

"Is she now?"

"Commander Paro arrived a short time ago with both in tow."

"Thank you Aeson. You may go now. I will go see Erinoth personally."

Aeson bowed and left. Rhys made his way down to the dining hall and opened the door. Erinoth and Raven were sitting at the table, eating. They both looked up to see the king and rose. Rhys stopped them with the wave of his hand and sat down on the opposite side of the table. He could tell they were both worn down from whatever trouble they had been in. Finally, he looked at Erinoth and spoke.

"It is good to see you again, Erinoth. I admit I was fearing the worst."

"Thank you, your Majesty. As was I."

Rhys turned his eyes upon Raven.

"Bounty hunter. I am curious why you are here."

"It was certainly not planned, your Majesty."

"I'm sure it wasn't. As eager as I am to hear what happened, I will leave you for now to eat and rest."

Raven and Erinoth both shook their heads and Erinoth spoke.

"My king, if I may."

Rhys eyed them and could tell whatever happened couldn't wait.

"Very well, but say nothing more until we are in a more private setting."

Rhys rose and walked to where Commander Paro was standing. Paro bowed.

"Commander, lead Erinoth and Raven to my meeting room. After that, make sure you and your men are well fed. I will order another garrison to replace you this evening. Take leave for the next couple of days. You've more than earned it."

"Sire, that is unnecessary."

"Oh, but it is, commander. Consider it my thanks for returning with Erinoth."

"Yes, your Majesty. Thank you."

Chapter Nine

Liam found his father in his meeting room speaking with a couple of his advisors. Warrick looked up and motioned his son inside. Warrick made one last remark to his aides and dismissed them. A strained smile formed on his face as he gripped his son's arm as Liam returned the gesture.

"Father, Evan told me what happened."

"It looks like your uncle is going to be a problem. He directly disobeyed an order, and the more I think about it, the angrier I get."

"Something about the bounty hunter Raven and the elf suspected of murder?"

"Yes. I wanted to speak to him personally to find out his side of what happened. I find it hard to believe the elves would break the truce between us. Well, Cameron apparently tried to intercept Raven and her prisoner, but they escaped. I was nearby when the guards were ready to give chase. I stopped them, but they were clearly not pleased with my order. Ever since your mom died, Cameron has harbored a burning hatred for the elves. Even I understand it was a terrible tragedy during a war that should never have been."

"Still, to go against your direct orders like that is treason. I love my uncle, but if it's true, that is unforgivable."

"I know, son. I've tried to give your uncle a good life in this kingdom, but his actions will eventually land him in the dungeon, or worse. You have always looked up to him, so I am trying to consider your feelings in all of this."

"Don't worry about me, father. I know you are trying to do what's right for our people. The war wasn't just destroying the Elven lands, but ours as well. Our citizens have lost so much in this conflict and now they have a chance to recover. Once we have a treaty in place, perhaps the nervous tension we all have will subside."

King Warrick placed his hands on Liam's shoulders.

"Thank you for understanding. My mind is more at ease now. Please keep your guard up if you are around your uncle. I don't know what he's up to, but I know he still wants a war. I'm afraid he will try something to undermine the treaty effort."

"I will have Evan monitor him. He has a good friend in Cameron's circle. I will see if he can make us aware of anything nefarious. He has no love for elves, but I don't think he wants another war either."

"Just be careful and make sure this person is trustworthy. We can't afford for something like this to happen again."

"Yes, father."

Liam gave a quick bow and left. Evan met him in the hallway and Liam asked him to talk to his friend.

"I'll talk to Theron and see where he stands before asking him to do anything like spying. I trust him, but he is loyal to Cameron."

"Be discreet. The last thing we need is for my uncle to find out we are watching him."

"Aren't I always?"

Evan followed with a hurt look on his face.

"It's like you don't know me at all."

Liam gave him a shove.

"All I know is you cheat to best me in sparring."

"Is that so? We may have to settle this with your father as the judge to prove once and for all it is you that cheats, my friend."

Liam laughed.

"We may just have to do this. In the meantime, talk with Theron and after that, perhaps we will ride out and see if we can find Raven."

Evan bowed in agreement and left.

*****

The next day, Evan found his friend inside the stables, working on a gate to one of the horse stalls. Apart from being a guard, Theron was also a handy carpenter; a skill he gladly donated since the stoppage of the war. Evan approached his friend and Theron gave him a hug.

"How are you?" Theron asked. "I think I saw you more during the war than I do now. Still babysitting the prince?"

"Well, if it weren't for me, he'd probably be dead by now."

"That I would not doubt. What brings you over to the stables? I'm surprised Liam isn't with you."

"I needed to talk to you about a private matter. That is hard to do with the prince in tow."

"Private, huh? Is Liam in trouble?"

Evan checked the stalls to be sure no one was inside.

"First, I need to know your thoughts on the truce. This is just between us, so please be honest with me."

"I think it was needed. The people are suffering."

"I know you are loyal to Lord Cameron. He wants to continue the war."

Theron shook his head. "I am loyal to our king. I respect Lord Cameron. He wants what is best for our kingdom, but I think he's wrong about wanting the war to go on. What is this about?"

"I think the king might be in trouble."

"The king? Are you certain of this?"

"Not completely. Which is why I came to you. Have you heard any rumblings from any of Cameron's men about a coup?"

Theron looked around to be sure they weren't being watched.

"You think Lord Cameron is planning to overthrow the king? Why would you think this way?"

"Do you remember the incident yesterday with the bounty hunter?"

"I heard a little about it, yes."

Evan shared the details with Theron.

He was genuinely shocked. "Why would Lord Cameron do something so brash? He's committing treason, if true!"

"Had it been anyone else, he probably would be in the dungeon right now. Cameron is Evaline's brother and uncle to Liam. The king still believes he can soften Cameron's hatred enough to accept a treaty between Sacia and Paelea."

"So, what do you need from me? I am assuming you have a reason for telling me these things."

"Yes, my friend. I just need you simply to listen for any threats against the king and report anything suspicious. I know I am asking a great deal from you."

"I will let you know if I hear of any plot against the king."

Evan clasped his hands on Theron's shoulders.

"Thank you, Theron. I will owe you for this."

Theron smiled. "You know it, and I plan to make good on that soon. In fact, there is a handmaiden I've been talking to, but she only sees me as a friend. Perhaps you could talk me up to her sometime? I don't have the skills with women that you do. Must have been something that rubbed off on you from Liam."

Evan laughed. "If anything, I might have rubbed off on him. He's always been awkward around the ladies such as you are. So, what's this handmaiden's name?"

"Lucy. She works over in the tavern."

"Don't worry. I will have you two married off by the end of the week!"

"Now don't go scaring her off, Evan."

"Just take care of what I asked, and I will put in a good word with Lucy. Deal?"

"Deal."

The two friends shook hands, and Evan headed back to the castle. Neither of them knew one of Cameron's agents was nearby. When he saw Evan slip into the stables, he approached and made sure either of the men couldn't see him. He overheard Evan's request to Theron and once he had heard enough; he slipped away to report his findings to Cameron.

Chapter Ten

Lord Cameron stormed into his private chambers. He should have known a friend to Evan could not be trusted.

"Fools! All of them!" Cameron cursed aloud.

He turned toward the agent. "Make certain Theron pays for his treachery. I don't care how you do it, but I want him dead, understand?"

"Yes milord, consider it done."

"Be sure it is and leave no traces back to me. Warrick already suspects I am up to something, which means I will need to move even more quickly now."

The agent simply bowed his head and left. Cameron paced around his room. What had been irritation at the king for halting the war now burned with hatred, and he could no longer tolerate a king who would cower to the enemy. That is what he considered the truce. Nothing more than a coward's way of ending a war instead of winning it and eliminating a filthy race from the face of the realm. He felt they had been so close. So what if the citizens were hurting? Once the war was over and Sacia was victorious, there would be more lands and riches to dole out. Now, that would never happen. At least not with Warrick or even Liam on the throne. He loved his nephew, but Liam held the same views as his father, and that was unacceptable.

It's a shame, really. If Liam was a little more open to my ideals, I would have more faith in him.

Cameron thought about his kingdom without a coward for a king. HIS kingdom.

Inevitably, people die in war. What a pity if Warrick and Liam fell victim to an uprising so that I could ascend to the throne and continue the good work that Warrick's father had started. What a pity, indeed.

Cameron knew Warrick was popular with the people, but not so with the nobles and the army. He already had most of the guards and a good portion of the soldiers on his side. The ones that sided with Cameron felt as those slain on the battlefield shed their blood for nothing. As for the people, they would come around and if not, he would force them to accept his rule.

Unfortunately, the situation with Raven and the elf escaping caused him to move up his plans for a coup. Unless the garrison he secretly sent out caught up to the fugitives and killed them, his latest treachery could be exposed, and that meant the gallows for him and his associates. No, he had no choice now but to put his plan into motion before that wretched king of the elves paid a visit to Warrick.

His pulse quickened as he thought of what was about to happen. He was going to kill the king and prince of Sacia. That should have caused him to hesitate, but Cameron now felt it was his duty to claim the throne and cleanse Paelea of its occupants. Yes, his purpose was noble in his mind, and it had to be carried out.

*****

Cameron summoned his most trusted allies and devised a plan. One of Warrick's bodyguards had already been bribed and was awaiting orders. Cameron would deliver them to the guard when he was resting. Once the guard returned to Warrick, he would wait for the right moment and stab the king with a poisoned dagger given to him with the orders. Right after that, he would send several of his finest soldiers to kill Liam and his bodyguard, Evan. Evan was poking around too much but in doing so, revealed Theron as a traitor. Unluckily for Theron, Cameron had eyes everywhere and when he agreed to Evan's request, Theron became disposable. Nothing was going to stand in his way now. The time had come for Sacia to return to glory. By this time tomorrow, he envisioned the king would be dead, along with his son.

Chapter Eleven

King Rhys sat back in his chair after hearing the accounts of both Erinoth and Raven. He was angry with Raven for capturing Erinoth to begin with, but ultimately understood she was just doing her job. He said nothing for several minutes, but finally stood.

"I need to speak with King Warrick directly and as soon as possible. Erinoth, I want you to come with me. If Warrick wishes to speak to you, then I will oblige him. He sounds as honest as I had hoped. Raven, you are free to go. I will pay you for bringing Erinoth back, even though that was not your original intent."

"Thank you, King Rhys, but that will not be necessary. I was going to turn him into Sacia for a crime he did not commit. It would not be right to accept payment from you."

"That may be true, but once you realized he would never see King Warrick, you risked your life to save him. That tells me what is truly in your heart. I will pay you. Don't insult me by refusing a second time."

"Of course, I will accept, your Majesty. Thank you."

Raven bowed, turned, and took the pouch that Aeson handed to her.

"Erinoth, it was… interesting to meet you."

"I do owe you my life, Raven. Perhaps we will meet again sometime."

"No offense, but I hope not. This entire ordeal has ruined what I do for a living."

"What will you do now?" Erinoth asked her.

"I need to see if I can somehow reach Warrick to explain what happened. He may already have a good idea, but my name is at stake, and I want to clear it."

"If you ever need anything…"

Raven cut him off. "Thanks, but no thanks. I'll be fine."

Erinoth, a little hurt, turned from her to follow King Rhys.

"Erinoth," Raven whispered.

"Yes?"

"Know that I appreciate your help in escaping."

"Same here."

Raven gave him a smirk, took one last look and headed out.

Just know we are alike, but you refuse to accept it.

The words from the mysterious woman spun inside Raven's mind. It wasn't until she heard those words that Raven started paying attention to what she thought were instincts. She always seemed to have the upper hand over all the other bounty hunters with capturing those running from the law. She could almost see into their minds to find their location or where they were headed. Now she began wondering who or what she was exactly. The woman unnerved her, but she couldn't show that in front of the woman and definitely not to Erinoth. It caused her enough distraction to where she almost walked right into a trap set up by Cameron and his traitorous soldiers.

Now Raven couldn't even seem to focus on what was right in front of her. She needed to reach Sacia and warn King Warrick just how dangerous Lord Cameron really was and what he might be planning. Instead, she wandered through the trees, focusing on who she was or wasn't.

"Damn you!" Raven said aloud at the woman, who wasn't even there. "Who are you to question who I am?"

"A witch, Raven." The woman appeared again out of nowhere and startled Raven... again. "That IS what you called me before, wasn't it?"

"Where the hell did you come from?" This time, Raven was not in the mood for her antics. That she snuck up on her again was unsettling.

"That's not important. If a witch is what you think I am, then a witch is who you are as well."

"Enough of this!" Raven pulled her crossbow from Shadow and aimed it at the woman. "Tell me who you are and what you want with me, or I will..."

"Will what?" The woman cut her off. "Murder me? I know you kill people for bounties, but I didn't know you could commit cold-blooded murder."

"For you, I'll make an exception."

"Please. You will need something more than a harmless grass snake."

Raven looked down and saw with astonishment as her crossbow transformed into a green snake. She dropped it immediately, and it slithered off into the bushes. Raven stared at the woman in bewilderment.

"What? The fearless bounty hunter startled by a little snake?"

"I just want to know who you are and how you think you know me!"

"So many questions. Why this? Who that? Why can you not accept the truth about yourself?"

"I don't even know who you are! All you seem to do is stalk me and ramble on about nonsense!"

The woman laughed at Raven. "I see it the other way around. You keep running into me. Maybe I should ask why you are stalking me?"

"I'm not stalking you!" Raven became furious. "I must warn King Warrick of Cameron's treachery! He may be in danger!"

"The king you speak of is in danger. In fact, before you even reach him, he will probably be dead."

"How do you know this?"

"After you left, I became curious. I disguised myself as a peasant and made my way to the castle and listened. I overheard some guards speaking of a coup. They are planning to remove King Warrick from the throne, and they have plants in the king's own bodyguards."

"You knew and did nothing about it?"

The woman laughed.

"I might be a… witch, but I am no god. I could have tried to reach the king, but then what? I admit, I might hold them off for a bit, but their numbers would overwhelm even me, and I would be dead. Then I wouldn't be here to help you."

Raven just stared at her for a moment and shook her head.

"Help me? A king is in danger, and you want to help me?"

"There is just no talking to you, Raven. I warned you before of darkness coming. I will need your help with that. We can't burden ourselves with senseless conflicts such as what's happening in Sacia."

Raven stood there speechless. She didn't even know how to respond at this point. Either the woman answered questions with questions or spoke in riddles. Raven's anger escalated. She was wasting valuable time standing there and arguing. The woman saw her frustration and simply placed a hand on the side of Raven's face.

"Sweetie, hatred is worse than a disease. Not only will it consume you, but it will also destroy you. The consequences will go far beyond oneself. It can destroy everyone around you and sometimes even people who you think you are detached from. You saved Erinoth and are now hurrying back to warn a king whose fate is sealed by his own actions. For what? To stop an inevitable war? The truce didn't stop the hatred of the Sacians toward the Paeleans. If anything, it just fueled it. King Warrick died the moment he offered the truce to Paelea. He just hasn't been killed yet. It doesn't matter though. When she comes, not only will Sacia and Paelea burn, but the kingdoms all around will burn as well. She will return to claim vengeance, and everyone will pay."

The woman dropped her hand from Raven and just stared at the horizon and closed her eyes as if to meditate. Raven was more confused now.

"She? Who is this 'she' you speak of? Or are you going to refuse to tell me this as well? Wait! Let me guess. She doesn't know who she is. Look, I've got to at least try to get to the king, and you are wasting valuable time."

The woman held her eyes closed longer and then opened them. She turned to look at Raven with a sad expression in her eyes.

"She… I do not know her name. I had a vision a few days ago when I was down by the same stream where you and Erinoth had stopped, and suddenly I was in her lair and saw her awaken. An aura surrounded her. I could not see who or what was causing it, but she was alive again. She looked as if she was listening to a voice. I listened intently and could almost make it out, but then it was as if my presence had been made aware and the voice was silent. The woman looked at me and said your name. She said to find you and that we were alike. Next, I was in a burning village and a dragon circled overhead. I awoke with my clothes singed from the fires in the village. Someone sent me a message. Therefore, I approached you, Raven. It is time you realize what you are. Raven, you obviously have powers, such as I. You need to learn to bring them out. You will be powerful, that I can sense."

"So let me get this straight. You had a dream that included a lot of crazy scenarios. Some random woman mentions a name that happens to be mine and you don't find this a little odd?"

"Do you know of another Raven in this realm?"

Raven pursed her lips. "No, but I'm not exactly in hiding, either. I'm well known in this realm. However, adding a dragon to your story adds a nice touch."

"You don't believe me."

"Not in the least. No offense, but you've wasted enough of my time. Whether you think I need to go to Sacia is none of your concern. If I may have my crossbow back, I'll be on my way. Feel free not to contact me again."

Elysia simply nodded. "I'll leave you be, but seek me out when you are no longer blinded. Perhaps it won't be too late."

Raven pulled Shadow to her and laying on the saddle was her crossbow.

"Thanks. I thought I would have to ride into Sacia with only my sword."

"You speak of toys when you have so much power inside."

"Yeah, sure I do. Goodbye, witch."

The woman watched as Raven raced off into the distance. She spoke out to Raven, though she knew she wouldn't hear:

"I cannot say to you who I am. If you don't believe me about you, you won't believe me about me."

Chapter Twelve

Theron was leaving the stables when the agent appeared in front of him.

"Hello, Luther. What brings you by?"

"Lord Cameron wishes to speak to you."

A knot rose in Theron's throat. *Calm down*, he thought. *He and Evan made sure no one was listening.*

"He does? Why me?"

"There's something that's come up and he needs your help."

"I will head there immediately, then."

Luther grabbed his arm and smiled.

"Before you go, I need something from you. Let's take a walk around back."

Theron thought the request sounded odd, but he knew Luther and considered him a friend.

"Okay, Luther. I don't want to take too long, as I don't wish to keep Lord Cameron waiting."

"Neither do I."

Luther's face turned grim as the two walked around behind the stables and out of sight. Theron saw two more of Cameron's agents. He began to get nervous.

"What is going on? Luth-"

Theron turned toward his friend just as Luther swung the blunt end of an axe against the side of Theron's head. The crunch of his skull was all that was heard, and blood splattered against the stone wall of the stable. Theron's body slumped motionless to the ground. Luther kicked him in the side three times and was satisfied the traitor was dead or would be soon. He motioned at the other two agents and directed them to dump the body somewhere outside the castle where the wolves would find him and make Theron disappear completely. Luther wasn't worried at this point if the body was found because by nightfall, no one would care about a missing nobody, anyway.

Amedee met Erinoth as he exited the king's chamber. Erinoth smiled at seeing the beautiful princess. He had long admired her but felt he could never stand a chance with the nobles that always came calling on her. He stared at her nervously. Amedee's long, blonde hair was braided down to her waist. She stood almost as tall as her father, and the resemblance between the two was striking. She was most definitely her father's daughter and deadly with a bow as well. He hoped to never see her angry, especially with him. In this moment, however, she smiled warmly at him and Erinoth soaked it in as long as possible.

"Erinoth, I am so grateful to see you returned."

"Thank you, milady."

Amedee shook her head at him.

"Please, just call me Amedee."

"Yes milad... I mean, Amedee."

She giggled at Erinoth and then linked her arm with his.

"Walk with me. I want to hear everything that happened. I knew those Sacians couldn't be trusted."

"I think the situation in Sacia is worse than anyone realizes. I think Lord Cameron might be planning something against their king. If he succeeds, the truce will be short-lived. King Rhys wishes to speak directly to Warrick, and I have requested to accompany him."

Amedee looked at him with surprise. "What? You wish to return to that place?"

"I do. Perhaps to help clear Raven's name as well."

Amedee stopped for a moment and looked at Erinoth.

"You and that bounty hunter seemed to have become well-acquainted."

Erinoth could not suppress the laugh that rose in him.

"If you mean by being captured, threatened, and almost killed, then yes, we became well-acquainted."

"Do you mock me, Erinoth?"

"No, not at all! I would classify our 'relationship' as mutual survivors. That is all."

"Well, I thought I saw something between you two, but perhaps I was wrong."

Erinoth was curious why she asked about him and Raven and pressed the matter further.

"Why ask me such a question?"

Amedee hesitated and backed away for a moment.

"No reason. I was only curious."

"Well, she barely even said goodbye when she left. Raven is not one to let anyone get too close. She also made it clear she hopes our paths never cross again."

"What a lonely way to live. I almost pity her."

Erinoth changed the subject.

"Amedee, you look radiant today."

"You are too kind, Erinoth. I wish you well on your journey, should you go. I will pray for everyone's safe return."

Amedee placed a quick kiss on Erinoth's cheek and linked her arm again with his and led him down the hallway.

"Would you mind escorting me to dinner this evening?"

Taken aback, Erinoth stammered out his reply.

"What? M-me? You want me to escort you to dinner?"

Amedee laughed at his reply.

"Yes you, silly."

Erinoth blushed. "Of course! I would be honored."

She stopped in front of the door to a guest room.

"Well then, you will find a suit laid out for you that would be perfect for tonight, just in case you said yes. I will leave you be and prepare myself. Should you need anything, I will have Portia wait nearby to assist you."

Amedee tightened her grip on his arm before letting go.

"It really is comforting to know you are back safely."

"I am glad to be back as well. I didn't know if I would ever see Paelea again."

"Well, enough of this talk. I must get ready, and so should you."

Erinoth bowed his head and watched as she disappeared around the corner.

What just happened? Erinoth thought. *Was Amedee really showing interest in me?*

His head was spinning, but he had no time to ponder such thoughts. He had little time to rest since he returned, but Amedee requested for him to be her dinner companion. Him! Erinoth opened the door to the guest room and observed the clothes laid out for him. *A bit much for my taste, but a small price to pay to escort a princess,* he thought. Erinoth just shrugged and began getting ready.

Erinoth stood outside his room, fidgeting with his clothes, as Amedee approached. Erinoth's jaw dropped as Amedee smiled and spun around in a blue gown with gold trim. Her hair flowed outward, and she stopped in front of him and fixed her hair before leaning forward and placing a kiss on his cheek.

"You l-look lovely this evening, princess."

"Well thank you, Mr. Oloris! Don't you look handsome this evening?"

Amedee giggled, and Erinoth took her hand and kissed it gently.

"We might be quite the scandal this evening, Erinoth. Do you still wish to come?"

I would only say no if it would cause you grief, milady."

Amedee laughed. "Nonsense, Mr. Oloris! It would honor me to entertain a scandal with you. Shall we?"

They locked their arms and strolled to the dining hall.

Gasps whispered throughout the hall as Amedee and Erinoth entered. Erinoth fought the urge to flee the room and instead held his head high and looked over at his evening date, who was smiling back at him. If she was nervous, she didn't show it. As a scout, he had learned to be swift and silent, but here in front of the nobles, he felt awkward and clumsy.

Amedee led him to his seat and curtsied to her father, who returned a nod and a smirk as he watched Erinoth out of his element.

The king rose and everyone rose with him. He proposed a toast in honor of his scout, who had returned after a harrowing ordeal. Erinoth blushed as he felt all eyes on him once more and raised his goblet toward his king.

Amedee whispered in his ear. "Looks like you're the guest of honor tonight. I'm glad I picked you to come with me."

Erinoth looked at her, and she smiled. Was that all this was? Was Amedee acting this way to convince him to come? Of course, she didn't feel the same toward him as he did for her. His head spun, and he felt like he couldn't breathe. The room looked like it was closing in on him. He backed up and stumbled over the chair.

"Are you okay, Erinoth?" Amedee asked, showing concern.

"Yes. No. I don't know."

Erinoth turned to King Rhys.

"My apologies, your Majesty. I'm suddenly not feeling well. May I be excused?"

Rhys frowned. "Are you alright?"

"I'll be fine. I… I just need to go."

Erinoth braced himself on the chair for a moment, excused himself to Amedee and hastened from the hall. Amedee looked at her father and he motioned for her to follow Erinoth. She apologized to the nobles and walked out after him. She caught up to him at the end of the hallway.

"Erinoth! Stop! Please!"

Erinoth stopped but would not turn around to face her.

"What happened in there? I've never seen you like this!"

"It's nothing, really. Just not feeling well, as I told your father."

"Look at me. Please."

Erinoth turned her way but stared at the ground. Amedee grabbed his chin and raised it up, so he looked directly at her.

"I'm sorry."

"Sorry for what? Acting a fool or leaving me alone in there?"

"Did you even want me there or were you just coaxing me as I was the guest of honor?"

Clarity came to Amedee, and she frowned.

"Of course, I wanted you there. You, being the guest of honor, were just my father celebrating your return. The people missed you. *I* missed you. I wanted you to go with me because I care for you."

Erinoth backed away and propped against the wall with his head down.

"I'm a fool. I was way over my head in there. I heard you whisper, 'guest of honor' to me, and I thought maybe that was why you asked me to go."

"That was a surprise for you, Erinoth. My father already knew I was going to ask you to dinner. Do you really think of me like that? Do you think of me as shallow?"

Erinoth saw the look in her eyes and knew he hurt her.

"Amedee, this has everything to do with me and not you. This was all so overwhelming, and I felt I didn't deserve this. In no way do I think of you as shallow, ever. I couldn't believe you chose me… and I'm just not used to the attention."

"You deserved all of it, but if I waited any longer for you to ask me to dinner, I would die an old maiden."

Erinoth didn't know how to respond. Amedee feigned an angry stare, and as he said something, she grabbed him and kissed him. His eyes went wide, but then relaxed and settled into the kiss.

After a few more moments, she pulled away and pushed a few strands of hair from her face.

"However, Mr. Oloris, if you insult me this way again, I may not be as forgiving. Until next time."

Erinoth bowed. "Until next time."

As Amedee walked away, she turned back to him. "I guess we gave them a scandal, after all. Goodnight Erinoth."

"Goodnight Amedee."

Erinoth stood for a moment and savored the kiss. As disastrous as the night had become, it ended on a much better note.

Chapter Thirteen

Warrick watched the sun fade away on the horizon. He pondered what real peace would look like in this part of the realm. He knew there would never be a lasting truce as long as Cameron was a thorn in his side. The king wondered if his brother-in-law had enough hatred for him to come after the throne. Perhaps he should have thrown Cameron in the dungeon for disobeying a direct order. He had shown his brother-in-law some compassion and hoped this would cause him to back down a bit.

The king did not know how deep the hatred ran through Cameron. He was also unaware the same guard stationed outside his door was awaiting the signal to kill him. As the day gave way to the approaching night, Warrick lit a couple of candles and sat down to read some poetry a citizen had given him a few days before. Perhaps this would relax his mind enough so he could sleep peacefully. After a while, his eyes got heavy, so he laid the book down on the table beside him and decided he would rethink his relationship with Cameron in the morning. King Warrick drifted off to sleep for the last time. He would be dead by morning.

*****

Darkness crept over the kingdom and what seemed to be just another night soon delved into chaos. Two guards walked up to the king's bedroom door, where the other two guards stood. Elliot, the guard who held the poisoned knife, greeted the other two. The guard who stood next to Elliot did not recognize the men from the king's royal protectors. He asked what they were doing there, and they simply replied they were to relieve them for the night.

"I received no mention of this. My orders are to stand here until dawn."

The guards standing before him looked at Elliot. Elliot nodded, and when the king's guard suspected something, it was too late.

Elliot stabbed him with the poisoned knife, just under the breastplate of his armor. The guard slumped to the ground. He could not even yell to warn the king. His last thought before slipping into unconsciousness was how he had failed his king. Cameron's guards pulled his body quietly out of the way. As Elliot gripped the knife, he began to sweat. Killing a guard was one thing, but the king? He quickly shoved those thoughts aside. Elliot had already taken the money, so it was him or the king at this point. He knew the guards were not there to protect him, but to ensure he followed through on his part. Elliot truly believed Lord Cameron would restore Sacia's glory by reigniting the war and winning it. He also shared the lord's disgust of the Elven people. All he had to do was finish this and Sacia would be strong again. So here he was, the plan falling into place. Elliot gently opened the door into the king's chamber and walked over to where Warrick lay. He cleared his mind of any doubts, took a deep breath, and plunged the knife into the king's side. He held it in and twisted as the king awoke and stared wide-eyed at Elliot.

"Why?" Pain spread quickly, and the king gasped for air. He tried to grab the knife but found he couldn't move at all. Blackness engulfed him as he just lay in bed, staring up at his royal protector. The king whispered one last word that was barely audible. Elliot could read the king's lips though: *Traitor*. Warrick's head tilted slightly to the side, with his eyes still wide, but empty. The king of Sacia was dead.

The look of horror was burned into Elliot's mind. He pulled out the knife, sheathed it, and ran to the door. He told the men waiting outside that it was done. The guards peeked inside and saw the king lying on his back, lifeless. All three then slipped away to report back to Cameron.

*****

Liam and Evan were having drinks in a local pub. They were talking with a couple of bards and laughing with the locals. With the stress of the previous couple of days, Liam decided against Evan's better judgment, and had a few ales. Make that several ales. Evan just wanted them to relax for the evening while they waited for any word from Theron. Evan found it odd that he did not see his friend here.

He must be out spying on Cameron or his men. Hopefully, he can find something out, so we know what Cameron is up to.

As Evan was thinking about his friend, he felt a slap on his back as Liam told one of his many tall tales. The prince was getting fairly drunk now so Evan told the barkeep to cut him off after one more. Evan only had a couple of drinks himself as he needed to stay alert for any threats against the prince. Liam gave a sulking look at Evan, and told the rest of the patrons his woman here wouldn't allow him to drink any more, obviously a mock toward Evan. The crowd laughed hysterically as Evan just rolled his eyes and shook his head.

Later that evening, Evan decided it was time to call it a night. He tapped his friend on the shoulder and pointed to the door. Liam nodded at his friend and said his goodbyes that seemed to take forever. Finally, they made their way out of the tavern and Evan helped to keep his friend on his feet.

"Remind me again why we're friends?"

Liam pointed his finger at Evan's chest.

"Because there is no one I would trust (hic) my life with. You are the greatest friend I've ever had."

"And probably the only one who would put up with you when you're this flipping drunk."

"(Hic) That too, perhaps."

They began walking toward the castle, and Evan saw a quick movement to his left.

"Who's there?" Evan called out.

He peered through the darkness but could see nothing. After a long moment, Evan got a bad feeling.

"I knew this was a bad idea tonight," he swore under his breath. *"I've got to get Liam somewhere safe and go check on the king."*

Evan knew one of Liam's hideouts was nearby, but he needed to be sure they weren't being followed.

"Let's go down this alley."

"Why?" Liam pointed at the top of the castle toward the right tower. "(Hic) You know we need to go up there? Are we headed to another tavern?"

"No, but I wish you'd sober up. I may need your help."

"What's going on?"

"I don't know yet, but I don't think it's anything good."

"I-I'm here for you. I can (hic) fight, just as well as you can."

Liam stumbled out of Evan's grip and pulled out his sword, waving it around. Evan got annoyed at his friend and grabbed his arm.

"You are in no shape to do anything right now but get yourself killed."

Evan pulled Liam down the alley leading to the side of the castle where the kitchens were located. He glanced behind and noticed a couple of shadows following at a distance. Evan cursed himself.

"Where are you, Theron? I could sure use some help right about now."

As they left the alley, Evan shoved Liam into a set of bushes that lined one of the kitchen's outer walls.

"Keep quiet Liam. I think we're being followed. I'll deal with them."

"I'm (hic) good. I'll help."

"You can barely stand. Just keep quiet."

Evan flattened himself to the wall next to the alley and when the men ran by, he stepped out into the open and pulled his sword. There were three of them, and they stopped and looked around. One man looked back and saw Evan.

"One of them's over here!"

Another spoke up.

"That's Evan! Liam's drunk, so he can't be far."

Evan knew immediately their lives were in danger.

"What's going on here?" Evan demanded.

"It's simple really, boy. We're gonna kill you and the prince!"

"On whose order?"

"Who do ya think?"

"Cameron! I knew it!"

"That's Lord Cameron to you, boy! It won't matter in a minute. We're gonna kill you like we took care of that traitor, Theron!"

"You did what?"

"Yep! Boss bashed his skull in, and we fed him to the wolves. He should be picked clean by now, I figure."

"You will pay for that!"

"I don't think so. You'll be dead right along with your prince."

"Then come and get me, cowards!"

"Let's get 'em, boys!"

All three men charged Evan. He blocked the charge of the first one and shoved him into the second. As both fell backwards, the third man came at him with a battle-axe. As he swung, Evan ducked under it and spun around and buried his sword in the man's back. He pulled it out just in time to block an attack aimed at his head. The two that were left attacked him at once, and Evan blocked each with relative ease. One pulled his sword around with both hands toward Evan's lower body and as he blocked that one, he felt a sudden burning sensation on his side. He spun around and two more joined the fray, and one man's blade was stained with blood. Evan knew someone had stabbed him in the side but wasted no time in checking the damage. By that time, Liam had joined the fight. Even drunk, he was still an excellent swordsman. Liam noticed the blood on the side of Evan's shirt and yelled if he was alright. Evan waved him off, and both kept fighting off the attackers. Finally, Liam struck down the last one as Evan grabbed his side and looked down at the blood on his hand. He knew he was in trouble.

Liam grabbed his friend and, even though still not himself, slipped into the darkness of night and made his way to one of his secret tunnels. He followed it out to the lake, where they had sparred just the day before. He let Evan drop to the ground and then fell himself. His head began pounding from the effects of the ale he had drank.

"I swear if we get through this, I'm giving up drinking completely!"

"You're such a liar."

Evan groaned, and he knew he was losing blood. Liam removed his cloak and ripped a piece large enough to wrap around his friend. He tore off another piece and walked over to the lake and soaked it in the water. He came back and cleaned the area of the wound. You're lucky. It looks like a glancing blow, but it's deep. Hold still while I wrap it. Evan grimaced as he sat up and raised his hands while Liam wrapped the wound.

"Some bodyguard I am. I had to be rescued by a drunk, know-it-all prince."

Liam laughed. "You did most of the fighting. I just helped you finish, and I am more than paying for that now."

Liam grabbed his head with both hands and laid back. "What do we do now?"

"We must get to your father somehow. He must be warned."

"If Cameron's coming after us, then he will surely go after my father. I don't know that we can get to him, especially like this."

"We must try. If Cameron gets to him…."

Liam shook his head. "I can't even think of that. Cameron would not kill my father."

"Liam, he just tried to kill you! The king is in imminent danger!"

"I don't think either of us will survive another fight, though. I know a way to at least get us close to my father's room. Let's go."

"Liam, I can't move that well, so if we're discovered, I won't be much help to you."

"Then we won't get caught."

Liam rubbed his head. "We should have seen this coming. *I* should have seen this coming."

"We don't have time to blame ourselves. Neither of us knew whatever was going on would happen so quickly. We need to go now, though, and find your father."

"Right behind you."

Liam stood up and helped Evan to his feet.

"If they don't know we're coming, we'll have the element of surprise."

"If they find the bodies we left behind, I don't think the surprise element will work."

"Then we'll force our way in. Even in our condition, we are still better than what Cameron will throw at us."

Evan nodded, and they headed back into the castle via the tunnels. After several twists and turns, they emerged into an empty hallway. As they scrambled up a stairway and through a maze of passageways, they finally came to the door that opened just below the king's bedroom.

Liam listened for a moment but heard nothing. Satisfied at the silence, they eased their way toward the king's bedroom. Almost immediately, Liam saw the guard slumped against the wall beside… the open door into his father's bedroom! Quickly, Liam darted into the room, and, to his horror, his father lay motionless, with blood dripping onto the floor. He rushed over to his side with Evan trailing and tears formed in his eyes. Seeing the pained expression on his face, Liam knew his father had seen his attacker, and that they had betrayed him. Liam cried on his father's chest and swore he would find Cameron and kill him.

Evan came into the room with a grim look on his face.

"It was Elliot."

"What? How do you know?"

"The other guard shared your father's fate, I'm afraid, and Elliot is nowhere to be found."

"It can't be! He was one my father trusted the most! They must have taken him!"

"There's no blood trailing off, and he's not here."

"Maybe he went after the killers?"

Evan just stared at Liam and gave a glance over at the king.

"I want to believe that Liam, but I can't. It was Elliot."

Liam placed his head against his father's and cried some more. Evan patted his old friend on the back and told him there was nothing he could do right now, and they needed to get out of the castle.

"I'll do no such thing! Cameron will pay for this and I'm going after him!"

"And do what? Take on all his soldiers? The only thing standing between Cameron and legally taking the throne is you. If you're killed, Cameron wins, and the entire realm will suffer, Sacia included."

Liam paced back and forth, still rubbing his throbbing head.

"I can't just let him get away with this! He must pay for what he's done!"

"And he will, but he has the upper hand right now. We need to regroup, heal up some and come back with numbers. It won't be easy, but it can be done, let's go… now!"

Liam cast a glare at Evan. Never had he snapped at him like that. The ale was still coursing through his body, keeping Liam off balanced and not thinking straight.

"Don't issue me orders, Evan. My father's dead, which makes me king now."

"Yeah, and when Cameron's men figure out we're here, you'll be a dead king."

Evan grabbed Liam and pulled him toward the door. Liam ripped his arm from Evan's grip.

"I will avenge my father and I will not wait!"

Evan looked at his friend and sighed.

"So, we die here then."

Liam shrugged.

"If we must."

Chapter Fourteen

Theron awoke and instantly felt a sharp pain at the back of his skull. He reached back and felt a knot along with matted hair which he assumed was dried blood. It was pitch dark, and he could hear howling in the distance. He knew the wolves would be here at any moment. Wherever *here* was. He laid there and looked at his surroundings. All he could see were trees. He slowly sat up, his head pounding. He knew he had lost a lot of blood and felt very weak. His eyes slowly adjusted to his night surroundings. Theron rolled over and raised himself up on his knees. He pieced together what had happened. He remembered Luther. They were talking. Something about Cameron.

What were we talking about?

He needed to see Lord Cameron. There were two other men there, too. That was all he remembered. They struck him from behind, but by who? Luther? He knew Luther was one of Cameron's top aides, but he also thought they were friends. Wait! He remembered speaking with Evan. He could barely think with the throbbing of his head. Suddenly, it hit him.

"Cameron might go after the king!" Theron said aloud.

Someone heard us talking! Theron thought. *We made sure no one was around, but obviously somebody overheard their conversation! What of Evan and Liam? Were they attacked as well? The king! Cameron IS going after him after all!*

Theron stood up but he could barely walk, and his head pounded with every step. After just a few feet, he fell. He had to get word to the king! Was he too late? Had he failed his friend?

Suddenly, he heard footsteps in the distance coming toward him. It didn't sound like an animal's footsteps. It sounded human. Did Cameron's men come back to make sure he was dead? Theron frantically looked around him but all he could see was the forest. Theron saw nowhere to run, not that he could anyway in his condition. He hid himself behind a tall, nearby oak and slid down.

He listened as the steps grew closer and closer. Theron slowed his breathing to not give himself away. The footsteps stopped in front of him. He listened intently.

"Theron Whittaker."

Theron glanced up upon hearing his name. His heart raced as he saw a woman before him, standing in a long purple robe.

"Wh-who are you? Have you come to finish me?"

The woman laughed.

"If my intent was to kill you, we wouldn't be talking right now."

"What do you want?"

"I guess I'm here to save you. You won't survive a night in these woods. I will, however, need something from you in return."

"Need something from me? I have nothing to give you."

The woman looked at him for a moment, and then a sly grin formed on her face, making him feel uneasy.

"What if it's your soul I crave? Hmmm?"

Theron froze. "M-my soul?"

"Yes, your soul. Apparently, Raven thinks I am a witch. What do you think?"

"I - I'm not sure what to think. Wait, you mean the bounty hunter?"

"Not anymore, she's not."

Theron could make no sense of this woman. He didn't know if she was here to help or to harm him. Either way, he knew he was getting weaker and propped himself up on the tree.

"Lady, my head is pounding and I'm losing blood. If I don't get help, I'm going to die out here anyway, so either help me or leave me to my destiny."

"You know nothing of your destiny, sweetie."

"You don't even know me. What would you know of my destiny?"

"I know enough, and this conversation bores me. Goodnight, Theron Whittaker."

"Goodnight? What do you me-"

Before he could finish his sentence, the woman engulfed his body in a purple mist that rendered him unconscious. She walked up and kissed him on his cheek.

"Such a handsome man. I have a need for you, but not in this condition. You will come with me."

She uttered a quick spell, and Theron rose off the ground in a horizontal position. The woman then left with Theron in tow toward her home.

*****

Raven rode all night to make up the time she lost by once again listening to the ramblings of a strange witch. Still, her convictions of a darkness coming unnerved her. She had heard tales in the past of a time when magic and dragons roamed the lands, but she thought of them as fairy tales. Now, she wasn't so sure. Shadow began breathing heavily, and Raven knew they needed to stop for a bit. She led Shadow to a creek and while her horse drank, Raven refilled her pouch. She surveyed the land around, halfway expecting that strange woman to reappear, but this time she didn't. Raven walked up and ran her hand down the neck of Shadow while she drank.

"I know you're tired, girl, but we need to keep going if we are going to have any chance of saving King Warrick. I'll give you a few more minutes and then we'll head out."

Raven stepped away from the creek and into the clearing past the trees. A grassy meadow stretched out in front of her. For the first time since tracking Erinoth, she allowed herself a moment to soak in the cool evening air. A not quite full moon hung overhead and allowed her to see in the dim surroundings. Off in the distance, she saw a sparkle. It appeared to be a campfire. Either soldiers still looking for her, or weary travelers settling in for the night. She did not want to find out, as Shadow was already tired from their hard ride throughout the night. Raven was pretty worn out herself. She decided they would take it slow for now so as not to be noticed by any nearby scouts. This would help Shadow recover some more as well. She walked back to her horse and saw a stranger holding on to the reins. Raven was not in the mood for marauders right now.

"Just what are you doing with my horse?"

"It's going to be my horse once I bring you in, bounty hunter. Or should I say, former bounty hunter?"

Raven cursed under her breath. She had been so distracted by the woman and the king that she didn't even realize she was being followed. She immediately recognized the man as a rival bounty hunter.

55

"You'll get your hands off her, Layton, if you know what's good for you!"

"Just what are you going to do? I have your crossbow right here with me. Come on, Raven. You're done. When I get you back to Lord Cameron, you will hang for sure. Should've handed that elf over. Now your life is over."

"Not if I have anything to say about it."

Raven dove to the ground and rolled. She could hear one of her own bolts just missing her head. As Layton scrambled to reload another bolt, Raven lunged to attack. She pulled a dagger from her belt and threw it toward Layton, but he reacted in time to block it with the crossbow. He tossed it aside and pulled his sword.

"Luckily, Cameron said to bring you in dead or alive. I'm going to enjoy killing you."

"You talk too much. I always hated that about you."

Raven stood back, picked up her dagger and placed it back in her belt, and drew her sword. Layton lowered his sword toward her.

"You might be better at tracking Red, but no one can match me in a fight."

"We'll see."

Layton attacked with a slice to the right side of her body. She blocked it with her steel gauntlet and launched herself past him, slicing his ankle as she went by.

Layton cursed as he spun around, limping on his left foot.

"I underestimated you, Red. That won't happen a second time."

Raven just smiled at him.

"You'll find I'm full of surprises."

Layton made a shorter swing this time and Raven tried his right side, but he blocked the attack, parried, and hit her arm hard enough to knock the sword from her hand. Her gauntlet again prevented him from slicing through.

Raven stood up and blew a strand of hair off her face.

Layton paced back and forth and then suddenly charged at her. Raven moved quickly to the side and shoved him down. He lost the grip on his sword as he hit the ground and it landed a few feet away. Raven pulled two daggers from her belt and plunged them into his back. Layton howled in pain as she twisted the daggers and then ripped them out. She stood up and calmly walked over to where his sword lay. With a grim smile on her face, she shoved his own sword into his back and into the ground. She watched as he lay there whimpering. He raised his head long enough to whisper that she was a dead woman, as he wasn't the only one looking for her.

"Good to know. Goodbye Layton."

Raven walked away as he took his last breath and slumped lifeless against the ground. She picked up her sword and crossbow, grabbed the reins, and mounted Shadow. She reached down and rubbed her side.

"We need to take it slow for a bit to make sure no one else is following, then we will make one last push for the castle."

Shadow neighed her response and off they went, slipping silently into the night.

Chapter Fifteen

Raven walked to the edge of the forest as it opened onto a prairie that spread for miles around. She tied off Shadow on the edge of a brook where she would have plenty of water. They had ridden hard into the next day with brief stops along the way, ensuring they were not being followed by any more bounty hunters.

Off in the distance sat the Sacian castle and its stone walls that circled the kingdom. Majestic in view, she knew that inside its walls were anything but. She would wait until nightfall to make her move. She needed to go over the plans she devised on the trip back from Paelea and needed the cover of night to help hide her presence from any nearby guards or soldiers.

Raven sat down by her horse and started eating some berries and roots she had picked up along the way. She realized she hadn't eaten hardly anything since she left Paelea, and her stomach was growling because of it. She closed her eyes and listened to the sounds of the day when she heard grunts and moans nearby. Silently, she grabbed her crossbow and snuck ever so silently to where the noise was coming from. She peered through a clump of bushes to find two men lying on their backs. From the looks of both, they were robbed and left for dead. They had cuts all over and their clothes were soaked with blood. Being cautious, she walked up to them and steadied her crossbow in their direction.

One man turned his head and looked at her.

"Lady, you might as well kill us. We don't have anything of value."

Raven recognized the voice.

"Aren't you the king's son? Liam?"

"Depends on who's asking."

The man just laid his head back and then turned back to her.

"Wait. I know you. You're the bounty hunter… Raven."

"Well, I was. Not sure what to call myself anymore."

Raven laid her crossbow down and checked him over.

"I hope the other guy looks worse. Who's your friend?"

"This is Evan, my bodyguard."

"Looks like you should hire a new one."

Evan tried to prop himself up but slumped back down.

"If not for me, the king here would be dead."

Raven froze at hearing those words.

"King? Does this mean what I think it means?"

"Yes, Cameron murdered King Warrick, and this one here tried to take on all of Cameron's men at once."

Raven shook her head at Liam.

"That was foolish."

"I was a little drunk… and angry."

"Even more foolish. It is a wonder both of you aren't dead."

"I'm not sure we aren't." Evan sighed.

"We escaped through the tunnels, but not before literally fighting for our lives."

Liam managed a small chuckle.

"Those idiots are probably still looking for us in the castle."

Raven looked up toward the castle.

"Which means once they're done, they will look out here. I guess my trip back here was meaningless."

"Meaningless how?" Evan asked.

"I tried to get back as quickly as possible to warn the king, but I guess my defiance moved Cameron's plans up."

"That also means he won't be officially on the throne until Liam is dead. He will come looking for us."

"Well, neither of you two can travel in this condition. We need someone who knows medicine. I will do what I can, but I'm no doctor."

"Perhaps I can help?"

Raven spun around at the sound of the voice and pulled out her sword.

"YOU!"

"Oh sweetie, put that away. You remember the last time."

"Go away, witch!"

"Still with the unpleasantries. You would rather these men die than have me help them."

"Help them? You'll probably just riddle them to death!"

"You know, you can be quite funny when you wish to be."

"I've had enough of you!"

Evan pleaded with Raven.

"If she thinks she can help, please let her."

Raven looked at Liam and Evan and looked back at her with a deadly stare.

"Liam is king of Sacia now. If you hurt them, so help me. I will kill you."

"Like you did that bounty hunter? I am aware of your anger, dear. Don't worry, I will fix them up like I fixed their friend Theron."

Evan sat up, ignoring the pain stabbing through him.

"Theron's alive?"

"Yes handsome. I found him in the woods on the other side of the kingdom. I guess someone wanted him dead as well."

The woman looked back at Raven as she continued.

"Seems like there's a lot of that going around these days."

Raven glared at her in disgust and walked off. She didn't trust the woman. Somehow, she seemed to know her every move, and that made her angry. Still, if she helped their friend, perhaps she wasn't completely evil. She was still a witch, though, and Raven wondered if *she* wasn't the one involved in all of this. Raven figured the woman was mad. She spoke in riddles and nonsense, yet she seemed dead serious when she spoke about her "destiny."

Raven suddenly realized she was in a trance and could not shake herself out of it. Everyone around her disappeared, and she stood inside the courtyard of the Sacian castle. The buildings were burning all around her and she looked down and saw red flames swirling around her hands. It shocked Raven that her hands did not burn from the flames. Guards nearby attacked her, and she roasted all of them with one wave of her hand. She then found herself in the throne room and Cameron was cowering behind the throne. Raven smiled as she thrust both of her hands toward the throne and a stream of fire engulfed Cameron, and he screamed in agony. Suddenly, she felt someone shake her from behind…

Raven snapped awake and found herself suspended above ground. The strange woman was shaking her. Raven fell to the ground directly in front of them. Liam and Evan just stared at her, wide-eyed and a little frightened. The woman just smiled at her, but Raven could see something in her eyes. She wasn't scared like the other two, but there was definite concern.

Raven turned and looked directly into the woman's eyes.

"Did you do this to me?"

"I'm afraid not, dear. This time it was all you. Your powers are growing, but I did not like the look in your eyes. You saw a vision and I can tell by your demeanor; it wasn't a good one. Was it her?"

"Who are you talking about?"

"The woman. Was there a dragon as well?"

Raven shook her head. "I don't know or understand what just happened. There was no dragon. Or another woman. It was just… me."

Raven shook the feeling away and gave the woman a threatening look. "Are you sure you didn't trick me, witch?

"Tricks? You suggest I am some sort of trickster? Like a jester in a court?"

"I don't know. You tell me."

"These men need my help or they're going to die. Do you really want that on your conscience?"

Raven relented and backed away.

The strange woman simply nodded as she engulfed the two men in a purple mist. With a twist of her hand, they rose and hovered in mid-air. She motioned for Raven to follow as they headed into the woods.

Chapter Sixteen

Lord Cameron walked up to King Warrick and poked him in the side with his sword. His brother-in-law was indeed dead. He asked about Liam's status and his commander told him Liam was seriously wounded but disappeared somehow.

"He's gone? You let him escape? He must not have been as injured as you say."

"Sire, he was bleeding out from several wounds. He won't last a day wherever he goes. We have instructed all healers not to assist him or Evan. I have men stationed at their rooms. They have no allies here."

"Then you best find his body. I cannot legally claim the throne if my nephew is still alive. I could force myself onto the throne, but the people would rebel in time. As it stands now, the elf returned and murdered the king and the prince. This will show the people I should be their rightful king. After that, convincing them to attack Paelea should be easy."

"Yes, milord. I already have men looking for him, but I will double the effort. We will find him."

"See that you do that, commander."

*****

King Rhys readied his men. He would visit King Warrick himself to show how serious he was about forging a treaty with Sacia, but he needed to know this was something Warrick truly wanted, and that Sacia was behind him on this. He understood Lord Cameron was a danger to him and to the Sacian king. Therefore, he brought his finest warriors with him. He sent Erinoth ahead to scout for any would-be traps. Rhys had originally refused to let his chief scout go, as Sacia's men would easily recognize him should they be still out looking for him. Erinoth reminded the king that last time he wasn't expecting anyone to be looking for him, but this time he would watch out for any potential traps. Rhys knew Erinoth was the best at what he did so he relented but did not like it.

The king called his protectors to him. He mentioned this was to be a simple peace mission but didn't know what they were heading into. Erinoth would report any dangers before they traveled too far into Sacian territory. He asked if anyone had questions and when no one spoke, he nodded to his commander. Paro gave the order to begin the trek toward Sacia. They were looking at a week's journey at a slow pace to show their intentions were peaceful. They did not want to give Lord Cameron any more reason to wage war against them. However, should war be inevitable because of treachery by Sacia, he would not hesitate to defend their lands once again.

*****

Three days without incident had the king feeling somewhat at ease. They did their best to avoid villages as they entered Sacia and the random people they came across didn't seem threatened by them. Once, the king motioned over a child who was half-hidden behind a tree. He asked the child what was wrong, and the young boy replied he was looking for some food for his sick mommy. The king gave the child some bread and jerky and wished good health for his mother. Further ahead at the bend in the road that turned west toward their destination, they looked out over a field where one of the last battles had occurred before the ceasefire. They could see scars from the battle and farms that lay in rubble.

Why would Cameron wish to restart a war that left both sides in shambles? Surely, their military is still suffering as we are. How can a man hate another race to where he forces other men to die for his insanity? How many of Sacian's citizens believe as he does? They must also be weary of war.

Beyond the grassy field rose another stretch of forest. Pine, Oak, and Maple trees scattered about as they passed. They approached another clearing and Erinoth was at the edge of the trees, waiting for them. He had set up camp nearby at the edge of a creek that paralleled the road. King Rhys asked if he had news for them. Erinoth nodded, but his face was grim. The king frowned and felt anger welling up inside.

"What is it Erinoth? What is wrong?"

63

"Your Majesty, I bring grave news. King Warrick and Prince Liam have been assassinated."

Rhys was shocked at the news. "Assassinated? Are you sure of this?"

"I am. I had settled in for the night near here. I overheard people passing by, discussing it. They were merchants passing through and had just come from the castle. From there, I made my way closer to Sacia, ensuring no one could tell who I was by keeping my cloak around me. I passed near a patrol and overheard them speaking about their deaths."

"I take it there's more?"

"Yes, my king. They are blaming me for it. They are saying the elf Raven brought in came back and murdered them."

King Rhys was quiet for several moments. He looked around and realized that people passing by stared at them and whispered. He looked at Erinoth with a grim look.

"This is unfortunate. No doubt without you, we would have ridden right into danger. We must now head back to Paelea and start preparing for a potential attack. I'm afraid our period of peace was short-lived."

Chapter Seventeen

Raven mapped in her mind the path that led to the house in front of her. The woman flicked her left wrist, and the door opened. She waved her right hand and Liam and Evan, hovering motionless, floated inside.

"Are they-"

"Dead? Hardly. Sleeping? Yes. It's easier this way if they aren't squirming." The woman motioned for Raven to follow and smirked. "Come in. I promise not to bite. You truly are a distrusting person, aren't you?"

"It's helped me survive all these years. If you don't trust people, they can't stab you in the back."

The woman frowned. "That's not a fun way to live." She moved the two men into another room and laid them down on a couple of blankets spread out on the floor.

Raven stared at the blankets and after the men were both laid down easily on them, she turned to the woman.

"You knew they were out there?"

"Of course! I sensed them when they approached."

Raven asked about Theron, and she shook her head.

"He wasn't nearby. I had to find him."

"Find him? For what?"

The woman brushed her off. "Again, with the questions. I bet half your bounties just gave up on hearing so many questions."

"You deliberately ignored the question."

"I have my reasons."

"Explain then."

"In due time, sweetie. I need to concentrate on your friends here."

Raven snapped. "No! I want answers now. How do I know you aren't doing anything nefarious to them?"

The woman just rolled her eyes. "Saving their lives is nefarious now? You really have quite the imagination, Raven."

Raven's anger grew. She looked down to find smoke coming from her hands. She raised them up to eye level and stared, moving her hands back and forth as the smoke continued to radiate from her skin.

"Are you doing this?" Raven demanded.

"No sweetie, I'm not."

The woman walked up and grabbed a hold of her right hand. It was almost too hot to touch.

"She knows who you are, Raven. You have a connection with her. I fear it's worse than I originally thought."

Raven pulled her hand away.

"Don't touch me, witch! What's wrong with me?"

The angrier Raven became, the hotter her hands were. The woman just stared at her hands and for the first time, Raven thought she saw a flash of fear in her eyes before the woman regained control of her emotions.

"I told you before, we are alike, you and I. Except your powers were locked away for such a long time. No one was around to teach you how to unlock and control them."

"You're not saying what I think…"

"What? That you're a witch?" The woman interrupted. "Well, I would say more like a sorcerer, but yes, a witch will suffice, if that's what you understand."

"What? No, it can't be! I am no one. An orphan who became a bounty hunter. Now you're telling me I have powers and that I'm a witch like you?"

"You see it with your own eyes, yet you still do not believe. It is dangerous for you not to have control. The magic could easily consume you."

The woman wanted desperately to tell her everything, but Raven was already angry and if her anger turned to rage, she might unknowingly kill everyone and everything around her. She needed to tell her when she was calm, and even then, she might need to place her under a calming spell to keep Raven's emotions in check. She would wait until Raven was asleep. Then she would cast her spell and awaken her.

"Who is this woman you keep referring to?"

"She has not revealed who she is just yet. I fear she will soon."

"You can't respond to anything with a direct answer, can you?"

"I tell you what I know, sweetie. It seems though, you are indeed a witch."

Hearing that made Raven even more angry. She held her hands out and realized both of her hands burst into flames, yet she felt nothing.

The woman took a step back. She realized Raven was losing control. Her anger was consuming her and by doing so, the magic inside her that had been held in check for so long, was pouring out. However, it was too much, too soon. The woman knew she had to calm Raven down, or her own magic might overwhelm her and hurt herself, or worse. She had wanted to wait to reveal herself to Raven. She knew that by doing so, more questions would follow. Those questions would reveal a secret she had held for so long. She would have rather waited to address that. Right now, though, she had to calm Raven down but if she used her magic, that might only cause her anger to intensify.

The woman sighed and looked at Raven. No sarcasm or quirky answers this time.

"Raven, you wish to know who I am. I know you think I'm mad, but what I am about to say is the truth." The woman hesitated for a moment and then continued. "My name is Elysia. I've watched you for a long time but dared not contact you. I have lived as you have, alone and independent. We share not just magic, but a bond as well."

Raven calmed down a little at finally hearing the woman's name. She stared at Elysia and could see fear in her eyes.

"A bond. You think we share a bond. You are mad."

"I've known this from people who looked after me as a child. They told me many things, most of which I cannot remember. One such thing that has stuck with me all this time was that I had a sister. An older sister who I had never known as they separated us when I was born for reasons I do not know."

Elysia knew she was misleading Raven about why they were separated. If she discovered the truth about her, Raven would surely hate her. For now, she would not tell her everything. Elysia could see calm returning to Raven as the fire that radiated from her hands disappeared.

"So, you think this older sister that you've never met is me? This is what you've been hiding from me?"

Elysia looked at her with tears forming in her eyes.

"Yes. That is exactly what I'm saying. We are sisters, you, and I."

Raven suddenly laughed, running her hands through her hair at hearing such a ridiculous claim from a stranger she barely knew.

"Look, I don't know what game you are trying to play with me. I have no sister, that I can assure you. I remember little as I was only a child, but I remember being hauled off to an orphanage because my mother died. There was no one else, certainly not you."

Elysia turned her head and Raven saw a single tear trickle down her cheek. Raven realized the woman truly believed they were sisters, but that wasn't possible. She remembered no one else in her life but her parents. Her father died not long before her mother had. He was coming back from town with the money he had made from the harvest when a group of men robbed and murdered him.

"I am sorry, Elysia, I truly am."

Elysia wiped her cheek but didn't look up at Raven. She just looked at the ground. Elysia swore she wouldn't tell her, but she felt she needed to know. She needed her trust.

"Raven, please don't hate me for what I'm about to say. I am the reason they sent you to an orphanage."

"You."

"I wasn't completely truthful with you."

"Shocking."

Another tear streamed down Elysia's cheek.

"The reason you don't remember having a sister is because I was the reason our mother died. She was with child and almost due, but something went wrong, and she delivered early. I made it okay, but our mother did not. She died giving birth to me."

Raven shook her head. "How do you know this?"

"The woman who took me in explained this to me when I was older."

"So, someone took you in and sent me to an orphanage? That's quite a story."

"You don't believe me."

"No, I don't. If this happened, as you say, why take you and leave me to strangers who didn't even care if I lived or died?"

"It had nothing to do with you, Raven. The lady who took me in barely had enough to feed herself. She couldn't take both of us. She told me she took me because I was a newborn and would have died in the orphanage."

"Well, lucky you. I almost died. I fought with the other kids almost daily and wondered often if I should just end my suffering. However, I drew strength from within to keep myself sane."

Elysia tried once more to reach for Raven's hands, but she pulled them back. She still didn't believe her, but at least she relaxed enough that her magic had subsided.

"Whether you believe me is irrelevant. The fact is, you have powers, such as I do, and you need to learn to harness it. I can help with that. You need me to help you."

"I've learned how to live on my own since my mother died. I will learn to control it myself."

Elysia's tone turned icy. "Do as you must. I need to finish tending to these handsome lads. They will need their strength for the battle that lies ahead. Be sure not to kill yourself, sweetie, or anyone else."

Raven watched Elysia for a moment. She rubbed her jaw before speaking once more.

"Since you seem to be actually answering my questions, I have one more for you. If you were taken in, how did you wind up alone in the forest?"

"The woman died when I was twelve. I was old enough at that point to know I did not want to go to the orphanage. The woman's heart failed her, so before anyone came by to check on her, I fled. I found an abandoned shack deep in the forest and made it into my own. I discovered my own powers when I came face to face with a grizzled bear. He charged me and all I could do was stretch my hands out, expecting to get mauled. Instead, purple flashes of light burst from my hands and engulfed the bear, killing her instantly. I was horrified, and I cried for days after that. Eventually, I learned to control my powers and here I am. Realize I was younger than you are now. It is harder to control it if you learn later in life."

"How do you know this?"

"I met another sorcerer, and he was about your age now. He too thought as foolish as you. He wound up being consumed by his own magic and died. I will leave out the gory details, though."

"Gory? What do you mean?"

"He exploded, dear. I had pieces of him all over my cabin and it took me a week to clean it up."

Raven wasn't sure if she was speaking the truth or just rattling on again. She couldn't tell.

Elysia changed back into a serious tone. "You're going alone, aren't you?"

"To the capital? Yes."

"Why? Why not wait for these men to aid you?"

"Because I can't wait that long. Cameron destroyed who I am. He will pay for that in blood."

"When will it be enough?"

"When will what be enough?"

"Killing, Raven. You hid behind your bounty hunter persona before, but that is history. You still crave taking a life."

"What I crave is vengeance for what he's done to me, Erinoth, King Warrick, and his son. Cameron cannot be allowed to restart a senseless war."

"Killing him won't stop any war. Lord Cameron might be the leader of the coup, but he leads men who carry his ideology."

"Perhaps, but he killed a king."

"And you feel it's your duty to fix it."

"Yes!"

"You're wrong. It's Liam's place to demand such vengeance, not yours. His father is dead because of his uncle."

"I don't care whose place it is. Leave me be *sister*. I will do as I wish, understood?"

This time, Elysia stood up, walked right up to her sister, and faced her nose to nose. Her eyes glowed purple.

"Do you have some sort of death wish? Are you looking to die?"

Raven backed up a couple of steps.

"No, I don't. I have survived this long on my skills and intuition."

"Have you taken on a full army before? That's what you will face this time."

"I already have a plan for that. Besides, part of my magic apparently is knowing something before it happens. Guess I'll just rely on that."

"There is no talking any sense into you, is there?"

Raven shook her head. She gathered her things together and headed for the door. As Raven opened the door, Elysia warned her: "I may not be able to help you should you find yourself in trouble."

"I never asked you to. Goodbye, Elysia. Be sure to look after these men."

Elysia nodded as Raven rode off. She watched her disappear through the forest.

"If you get yourself killed, this realm is doomed."

Chapter Eighteen

Raven disguised herself in peasant clothing and rubbed dirt on her face to help disguise her appearance. She knew she risked her life to hunt down Cameron within the castle walls, but felt she had no choice. Between her reputation, Erinoth, King Warrick, and Prince Liam, she had to try. She couldn't wait for Liam and Evan to heal. Right now, the kingdom was in chaos, and she knew this was the best time to sneak in without being noticed. Also, Cameron might feel all threats have been dealt with. He might even think she tucked her tail and ran after fleeing the capitol, so she might not even be on his mind at this point.

Raven gently caressed Shadow and, almost in a whisper, told her to return to the woman they just left and slid a note where it could be seen by Elysia.

"She might be crazy, but I don't think she would harm you. You should be safe there. You're too noticeable to go with me now."

Shadow neighed at Raven and rubbed her head on Raven's shoulder. Raven let out a chuckle.

"I'll miss you too, girl. We'll see each other soon." Under her breath, she muttered, *"I hope."*

Raven clicked her tongue and tapped Shadow on her side. The horse hesitated, but then began heading back to where they had just come. Raven watched her for a minute and sighed. There was no going back now, even though her senses screamed at her not to go through with her plan.

*****

Raven met up with a caravan and asked if she could accompany them. She told them she was recently widowed and was going to the castle to look for work. They obliged, and she blended right in with them, and she kept her head down as they approached the gates. Raven looked up for a moment and noticed the guards were the same ones who had chased her out days before. She gripped her dagger tight inside her cloak. She had to be ready for anything.

As Raven passed by, one guard grabbed her by the arm. She fought to keep her calm and just released a gasp.

"What is your story, sweetheart? I don't see a man with you. Why not meet me at the tavern later for a drink?"

One woman she was with pulled her away from the guard.

"Please, have some respect, sir. She is recently widowed and is still grieving."

At first, the guard stepped toward the woman but was pulled back by the second guard.

"Leave them be. The lady's grieving. I'm sure you can find a nice wench at the tavern."

The first guard grunted his displeasure but finally relented. "Move along. When you're done grieving, come find me. I'll take your mind off your troubles."

Raven only nodded and stuck close to the woman that helped her.

"These guards have turned nasty, and it's just been recently. They must be spoiling to fight after that elf killed the king and his son."

Raven looked at the woman. "The elf?"

"Yes. He escaped with a bounty hunter several days back. Must have snuck back in somehow."

"You think they mean to restart the war?"

"That is what Lord... I guess he's King Cameron now... told everyone. The Elven assassin killed both King Warrick and Prince Liam. They went after him, but he got away."

"Hmmmm... Guess we were lucky King Cameron could escape harm. This kingdom might have been in real turmoil with no obvious heir."

"Yes. We're very lucky, and I hope he destroys that filthy race this time. I don't know what King Warrick was thinking. His own naivety betrayed him. His love of the elves led to his downfall. I hope our new king will be a stronger leader and lead Sacia into prosperous times."

"We can only hope." Raven thanked the woman and everyone else from the caravan. The woman gave her a hug and asked for her name. Thinking quickly, she told them she was Elysia.

"Elysia. What a pretty name. I'm Calina. Perhaps we will see each other again soon."

"Perhaps. Thank you again for your help."

"This is such a hard time for you. If you ever need a friend, I will be set up in the market."

"I will keep that in mind." Raven received one last hug from the woman and then watched them leave. She wondered how people could live accepting everything they heard as facts. Calina, as nice as she seemed to be, took Cameron's words to heart and wanted vengeance on the elves. She looked around the courtyard and wondered how many more believed the traitorous liar.

As she walked toward the tavern, she listened intently to the people that passed by. Some wondered to themselves about where the kingdom will go from here. How an assassin got so close to the king, and when the new king will retaliate to avenge Warrick. She heard so many questions without answers, but the one thing she deducted from it all was that the citizens were scared. Scared from losing their king. Scared of the uncertainty of the future, and scared they may lose their homes and loved ones because of another war. The last one was ironic as they had all celebrated the cease fire so that they could reunite with loved ones, alive and dead. Now, they were demanding another war with the elves.

No wonder evil kings rise to power, Raven thought. *They can easily manipulate the average citizen to believe or accept anything these tyrants declare.*

I know Elysia spoke of some type of darkness coming, but I can no longer ignore what is happening around me. Erinoth might have cost me my life as a bounty hunter, but I can still use my skills to stop Cameron. I only hope I can control my anger so that whatever's happening to me doesn't spiral out of control. I still can't believe she thinks she's my sister, but I also can't deny what she has told me so far is the truth... so far.

Raven still could not trust Elysia. She still saw her as some crazy witch who has lived out on her own for too long. Raven would have to figure all of that out later, though. She had a job to do.

As she approached the tavern, she sensed someone following her. Was it her newly discovered powers? It could have simply been the years of survival that honed her senses. Either way, she needed to find out why she was being followed. Surely, Cameron couldn't know she was here. Even the guard that questioned her never got a good look. Still, she needed to be cautious. As she neared the door to the tavern, she passed it and walked around the corner as if she had changed her mind. She hid behind some shrubs until the stranger walked around the corner. It was obvious now. She was being followed. As the stranger approached the shrubs, Raven sprang from her hiding spot and pinned the stranger to the ground. Her dagger was against the guy's neck, with her other hand over his mouth.

"Who are you, and why are you following me?"

She removed her hand from his mouth but kept the dagger against his neck.

"Scream and I slit your throat, understand?"

"The name's Luther, and I have no intention of screaming, bounty hunter."

"You know who I am?"

"Of course. You may think King Cameron is so inept as to not think you would eventually come after him, but he was actually expecting you. That was a nice disguise you used, but the guard recognized your voice even if he didn't see your face. I was to trail you to be sure it was indeed you."

"So, you have. Unfortunately, you won't live long enough to tell anyone."

"I don't think you understand, bounty hunter. I am only a distraction."

"What?" Raven looked up to see a club swinging toward her. She ducked just in time and the club sailed over her head. Luther took advantage and kicked Raven backwards. She stumbled and as she tried to regain her balance, the guard clubbed her on his second attempt, and she was unconscious before she hit the ground.

Luther checked her head. "She'll be fine. Make sure you bind her well. None of us wants to return to King Cameron empty-handed this time."

"Yes, sir," the guards chimed in and made sure Raven was tightly bound. The biggest one threw her over his shoulder and headed toward the castle.

Chapter Nineteen

Liam woke first and expected his whole body to hurt, but as the grogginess faded away, he found he had no pain. He checked where all of his cuts and bruises had been, but they were all gone. He looked over and saw Evan asleep. At least he hoped he was asleep. He looked to be healed up as well. Wait, where were they? Liam sat up and looked around. He remembered making it to the woods outside of the castle, and then he remembered a woman. She was helping them. Was it Raven? No, wait. Raven was there, but there was someone else. Someone he didn't know. The last thing he remembered was seeing purple all around him, and then he woke up in this room. How did he get here? Did the woman kidnap him? Where was Raven? He rubbed his forehead and spun around at the sound of a voice.

"Good morning, sunshine! Welcome back to the land of the living."

"Who-who are you and what is this place?"

"You like questions too, it seems. People in this realm talk and talk, but never take time to listen. Listening is how you learn. Not talking to hear yourself think."

Elysia shook her head. "I am the one who saved you and your bodyguard."

"Did you say we were brought back from the dead?"

Elysia laughed. "Almost, but not quite. You both have a strong will to live. I'll give you that."

"What about Evan? Is he okay?"

"He'll be fine. Your friend was a little worse off than you, sweetie. He may be out a little while longer."

Liam looked down again at what were his injuries. Only scars remained.

"Wait! This is impossible! How did…?" Liam slid back a little from the woman. "What did you do? Is this some sort of magic?"

"Some sort, yes. Would you like me to return you to how I found you, prince?"

Liam felt uneasy. "What do you plan to do with us?"

"Hmmm… I hadn't thought that far ahead. You know, us witches tend to eat their prey. Perhaps I am keeping you healthy until I get hungry."

Liam stood and looked around for any sort of weapon. Elysia simply laughed at him.

"Settle down, sweetie. I said that in jest. I don't actually eat people. So, tense! Come now, you need to eat."

Liam hesitated, and Elysia rolled her eyes at him.

"If I meant you harm, I would have just left you out there to die at the hands of Sacia."

"And what of Raven? What have you done with her?"

"Raven is off trying to get herself killed, I suspect. My sister doesn't seem to be the most stable person."

Liam shook his head. "You never told me who you are. How is Raven getting herself killed and wait, she's your sister?"

Elysia sighed and looked Liam right in the eyes.

"I give you answers but you simply ask more questions. Are you certain you and Raven aren't related?"

"No, Raven and I are not related." Liam lost patience. "Who are you? I won't ask again."

"Yes, you would. I'm bored with you, though. Who am I, you ask? I am someone you would never see, but I might be right beside you. I try to balance the evils in this world by doing some good in it. By looking at your expression, though, I assume you wish to know my name instead. I am Elysia. I am a sorcerer of sorts, but if you ask my sister, she will just tell you I'm a witch. She seems to think I'm a little odd as well. Aren't we all odd, though, in our own way? Oh, and I think she's going after Lord Cameron for killing your father and ruining her life, though her life is just beginning, and she won't even see it."

Liam's head spun at her words. The only thing he responded with was, "How do you know this?"

"My apologies for being so blunt on the matter. I assumed this was the reason I found you almost dead in these woods. Word has spread among the peasants that you and Warrick were dead, and that Cameron has assumed the throne."

"He killed my father. We wound up like this going after

Cameron."

Elysia shook her head and leaned in toward him. "Are you sure you and Raven aren't related? You both seem to have a death wish."

"No, we're not!" Liam fell silent for a moment. "I just can't believe my uncle would betray us. My father welcomed him into the family, even after my mother died. My father gave him land and a title. I guess none of us saw the evil behind his eyes."

"None of us can see the evil that lies inside of others unless they want us to see it. Sometimes you can see a little of it in an unexpected moment. We all have it inside, but most can control it or push it so far down that it never sees the light of day. This uncle of yours, though, has opened the blinds to his soul and unleashed a fury that cannot be satisfied. War is coming, prince. However, that will pale compared to what lies beyond."

Elysia looked down and saw Evan stirring.

"Never mind that for now. I see your bodyguard is waking up. You may wish to catch up on things with him. I will go tend to Theron as he was a little closer to death than you two."

"That's right!" Liam exclaimed. "I remember now you mentioned Theron before. How is he? May I see him?"

"He's resting. Deal with your friend, prince, and once he has fully regained his senses, you can see your friend. You will need him. I'm sure you wish to avenge your father."

Liam stopped for a moment as those words pierced his heart. *Avenge your father.* His father was dead. He didn't want to believe it, but he saw him with his own eyes. Now Raven was going alone on her revenge quest. *Why didn't she just wait for us?* He didn't know what magic Elysia had, but he had to admit he was feeling like new. If she was some dark sorceress, she was hiding it damn good. Plus, she helped Theron as well. He turned as Evan sat up, looking confused as he had a few minutes ago. He looked around at the unfamiliar surroundings and then spotted Liam.

"Where are we?"

"We are at that woman's home, the one who found us. She has been healing us."

"I remember Raven being there with us," Evan said.

"Apparently they might be sisters, but I'm not sure I trust this one."

"Well, she didn't kill us. That's a plus for me."

Liam nodded. "True, but she's rather strange."

"I remember she mentioned Theron. Where is he?"

"Slow down, Evan. Give yourself time to gather your senses. He's here apparently, in another part of the cabin. At least, that is what she told me. He's bad off."

Evan looked down at where his injuries were.

"How? What? Who is this woman?"

"Keep it down. She seems okay in that regard. She said we can see him in a few."

Liam's eyes turned cold.

"Raven went after Cameron."

"She did what? She went alone?"

"Yeah. This woman — her name's Elysia, by the way — asked if we were related because of that."

"Well, you both seem suicidal."

"At least I can blame mine on drunkenness. She apparently left sober."

"I don't think being sober would have stopped you last night. At least we tried. We were so close before reinforcements came."

"Not close enough. What I wouldn't have given for a bow last night. I would have put an arrow right through his heart!"

"Perhaps Raven will take care of him for us."

Evan changed the subject.

"How long have we been out for?"

"I don't know. Long enough for word to get out, I guess. Sacia thinks I'm dead as well."

"If not for your tunnels, I'm sure we would both be dead."

Evan checked himself again, shocked at how quickly his body had healed. Liam sat down by his friend.

"We need to help Raven."

"I figured as much. What's the plan?"

"I don't know yet."

Liam looked up to see Elysia by the door. She motioned for them to come in where Theron was. Liam didn't know him very well but knew Evan and he were good friends. They both walked into the room where a purple glow surrounded Theron. He looked dead lying on the bed with his arms beside him. Evan looked at Elysia.

"He's alive?"

"Yes. When I found him, he was almost gone. Between you three,

I'm exhausted. Using magic takes energy. To heal, it takes more energy. Once the haze dissipates, he will awaken. After that, he will be weak. You are welcome to stay as long as you need. However, I can sense Raven is in danger. She will need your help. I cannot go, as I need to rest. I would be worthless to you in this condition. Once I awaken, I will look for you, prince."

"Thank you, Elysia. We owe you so much for healing us."

"I'll keep that in mind." Elysia smiled at them and retreated to her room.

Evan looked at Liam. "What did she mean by that?"

"I don't know, but let's not worry about that now. Let's see how your friend is."

They walked into the room and watched Theron as he slept. There was no sound coming from the field that encompassed him. It appeared almost as an early morning mist that rolled through the valley. Not quite a fog, but close. They both reached out to touch it but pulled their hands back when they felt it tingle. Better not tempt fate, they decided. They watched for almost an hour and then Evan noticed it got thinner. He bumped into Liam, who had fallen asleep in the chair beside him.

"It looks like it's subsiding."

They stood close by until the mist was gone and after a little while longer, Theron stirred. Once he opened his eyes, he saw two individuals standing by him. His eyes were blurred, so he asked who they were. Evan told him where he was, sort of, as they really didn't know either. He looked at them with a worrisome look. Without knowing how long he'd been asleep, he shot up and grabbed Liam's arm.

"Liam! I must tell you something! Lord Cameron plans on killing the king!"

Chapter Twenty

Raven awoke to water being splashed on her face. She was bound by chains to her arms and legs. She looked around and realized she was in a dungeon cell. The side of her head throbbed, and her vision blurred. She winced in pain as they splashed water on her again from outside of her cell. As her eyesight slowly came into focus, she recognized the man staring at her. *Luther, wasn't it?* He was the one who had followed her, and she walked right into a trap. What an amateur mistake, and one she was paying dearly for.

"Well, the bounty hunter has finally awakened. Our king was concerned we had killed you before he could torture you."

Raven lifted her head up. "It probably would have been better for him if you had killed me."

"Such brave words from someone chained in a dungeon. Don't worry, we're still going to kill you, but King Cameron wishes to see you first."

"So, Warrick is dead. Cameron is no king. He's nothing more than a coward."

"Watch your mouth, woman! King Cameron is the rightful heir to the throne after the elves assassinated King Warrick and Prince Liam."

"You say that like you believe it. I know I ruined his plans to trick King Warrick into another conflict with Paelea. His hand was forced, and he had to make his move before the king banished him from Sacia."

"That's an interesting story, bounty hunter. Did you recite it to yourself to make it sound more convincing? You are a traitor to Sacia and the kingdom will know it come tomorrow."

Raven's head pounded to the point where she couldn't say anything else. She suddenly became nauseous and vomited on the ground below her. Dizziness set in and she closed her eyes for a moment, trying to force the nausea to stop. She looked up at the man and tried to utter a response, but she passed out before she could speak. Luther told the guards to leave her be.

"We'll wake her up again when the king comes to visit." He looked at the woman with disgust. "Pathetic. With her reputation, I expected more of a fight. King Cameron will make an example of her and let it be known he will not tolerate unruly behavior."

Luther turned to leave but looked back over his shoulder before exiting. "Keep a close eye on her. If she escapes, I will hold you two accountable."

"We'll watch her every move. She won't be going anywhere!"

Chapter Twenty-One

King Rhys ordered his top officials into the planning room. Princess Amedee was there, as was Erinoth. The king asked Erinoth to inform everyone of what he had learned. Erinoth nodded and reported about King Warrick and Prince Liam's death. He explained how Cameron had taken hold of the throne and would no doubt launch an attack against them. When they would do so, was the question. Commander Paro spoke up and said Cameron would be a fool to attack at this point. The elves had done a much better job of recovering, yet keeping ready for any attack, whether it be from Sacia or one of the outlying kingdoms. King Warrick had no desire to restart the war and had given his army leave while retaining a small contingent to stand guard for show more than anything else. This, Commander Paro pointed out, left Sacia vulnerable.

Rhys listened to his commanders. Vaeril, commander of the northern army, proposed striking now while Sacia was vulnerable. He pointed out that surely, the armies of Sacia were unprepared for an attack at this point. They could go in, take control of the kingdom until it was decided what to do next. Rhys asked what would happen should the citizens reject their control of Sacia. They were already under the assumption the elves had killed their king and his son. Should they attack and kill or capture Cameron, this would not sit well with their people, and they would outright revolt. There didn't seem to be an obvious solution to the unfolding of events. Should they sit tight and wait for Sacia to rebuild their armies? Or take the fight to Sacia and then deal with a citizen's revolt? Either way, both sides lose. The only outcome that might guarantee Paelea wasn't annihilated was for them to go on the offensive. It would be difficult to defend both cities in the short term, and they could not ward off threats from other kingdoms in the realm.

Paro came forward and suggested recruiting locals to join the army. They could plead with them to be guardians of their homelands, while the more seasoned soldiers could attack and hold the Sacian stronghold. As the new recruits became better trained, they could be added to the regular army. Other commanders chimed in with their ideas and Rhys listened intently to everyone. Once he had heard all he needed to hear, he raised his hand and asked for silence.

"Thank you for meeting here today. You all raise valid points, and I will take into consideration everything you have said in my final decision. War is not something we should just rush into. It's possible King Cameron will double his efforts to get his soldiers ready for an all-out assault on us. I will decide our plan of action in a day or two. I promise it will be no longer than that as I understand the urgency of the situation. Sleep well and I promise I will do everything in my power to ensure Paelea lives on and prospers despite the evil intentions of others. You are all dismissed."

Princess Amedee approached her father with a look of concern. "Father, is this Cameron really so evil that he would try to exterminate an entire race of people?"

"I do not know Cameron personally, but from hearing Erinoth and Raven's accounts of their dealings with him, it would not surprise me at all. You take someone who longs to finish crushing his enemy and then have that finality taken away, one can become vengeful. Add to that the evil that lies hidden, and he becomes a monster. There is no reasoning with a person such as Cameron. All it takes is a moment for that evil to find its way to the surface. From there, it will lash out and people and nations will suffer."

Rhys saw the horror in her face and gave her a comforting hug. She had made him promise years ago that he would hide nothing from her, no matter how bad. He hated to tell her this, but he would not lie to her either.

"No need to worry yourself with this. Our commanders all have great ideas, and whatever I choose will be a solid strategy to win. You understand that a man like Cameron will use his anger to attack and conquer, but it's that same anger that will make him reckless and sloppy. Warrick and his father before him were excellent strategists and constantly thwarted us when we thought we were gaining the upper hand. Therefore, we struggled so hard to defeat them. They were smart and patient with their decisions, whereas I predict Cameron will be impatient and will expect a quick victory. The longer it takes for him to realize his goals, the more demanding he will get. He will then make rash decisions that will get his men killed. Make no mistake, though, we will not be overconfident when we deal with Sacia. We will be precise in our execution and determined as warriors. Paelea will live on."

"Will there be room for me to join you in battle, father?"

Rhys shook his head. "I need you here, should anything happen to me in battle. You are more than capable of handling yourself; I know. But if both of us were to die in battle, there would be no one to assume the throne and it might force Paelea into a similar position that Sacia is in now. As before, you will be in charge of our defenses here. Should a surprise attack hit while I am away, I have all the confidence in you to defend our homeland."

"I understand, father. I will pray for our safety, but we will be ready should trouble come."

Rhys smiled. "I know you will."

"Does this mean you've already made your decision, father?"

"Yes. I do not wish for war, but Sacia will come after us. I would rather hit them now while they are at their weakest. It won't win us any favors with their citizens, but I need to think of our people first. War is truly Hell, and someone must lose. Sometimes, there is no winner at all. I fear this will be one of those times. Still, it's a decision I must make and must live with. God help us all."

Chapter Twenty-Two

Theron sat on the side of the bed and was processing what Evan and Liam had told him. He was supposed to warn them should he discover anything. He should have known they were overheard. Even though they were in the stables, he should have assumed someone might still be within earshot. He should have run the moment he suspected Luther knew. If, but, and why, all ran through his mind. They almost killed him. He should be dead, even now. What sort of magic brought him back? He hadn't heard of magic being used by anyone in his lifetime. Now he was in the house of someone who saved him with magic. Why him? He was no one special. Evan tried to ease his mind, but he kept running the moment they caught him over and over in his mind. Theron thought he and Luther were friends. Now, he realized just how deep Luther's loyalty to Cameron really was.

Liam paced the floor, thinking of what they should do next. Raven was more than likely in trouble, or worse. She wasn't normally reckless, but he felt she might be desperate to reclaim her name by seeking vengeance. Elysia was an option, but he did not know when she would awaken. Liam didn't know her well enough to wake her and explain they didn't have time for this. He didn't know how she would react. He already viewed her as unstable. Serious one moment and calling him sweetie the next. No, they were on their own. Unless…

Liam stopped pacing and looked at Evan. "What if we go to King Rhys?"

"That might not be a bad idea, actually I'm sure he has heard the news by now."

Liam nodded. "He's more than likely shoring up his defenses. I don't think he would outright attack Sacia at this point."

Theron finally spoke up. "If he was as smart a king as we all think he is, he would attack Sacia now. King Warrick had put most of the army on leave. There's only a small garrison officially active."

Evan nodded. "You may be onto something. He trusted King Rhys not to attack during the ceasefire and King Rhys had verbally agreed to an official end to the war. If Rhys has heard of what Cameron has done, he should attack, knowing full well of Cameron's feelings toward the elves."

Liam thought for a second. "You know Evan, I hate when you're right."

"It's a gift. You must hate me a lot."

"I find you more annoying than anything."

Evan merely shrugged as Liam continued.

"King Rhys should know if he attacks without cause, the people of Sacia will wholeheartedly rally behind Cameron. We will lose all the work my father did to forge a lasting peace between the two kingdoms. We must head to Paelea and either plead our case or hopefully catch up to them before they reach the Sacian border. If he realizes I am still alive, perhaps that will buy us time to figure out how to remove Cameron from the throne and to create an ally with Paelea."

"Count me in." Theron remarked. "As soon as I get my legs working right."

Evan patted his friend on the back. "We all need to gain our strength back. Let's see if Elysia has any food stored around here. I assume even a sorceress eats."

Liam nodded. "She's human, just like we are. She just somehow possesses magic that we can't."

"Whatever you say, prince. She still creeps me out."

"That I will agree on. Let's get some provisions and get out of here, wherever here is."

✶✶✶✶✶

Mother! What are you doing here? I thought you were dead.

That's just what you were told, my child. I had to go away for a while. People didn't know who I was or what I was. Had they found out, they would have killed us all. Once people became suspicious of me, I faked my death to save both of you.

Why are you back now? Do you really think after all these years I will just forgive you?

You will, in time. Elysia has.

86

Elysia's crazy. There is no way I'm coming with you. I have my own life here.

A life that's been destroyed. Besides, you say that like you have a choice.

I have a choice, mother. Just let me be and take my sister with you.

I'm afraid I can't do that. I need you to complete the ritual.

What ritual? Never mind. I don't want to know. Leave now or I will make you leave.

Oh, child. Always disappointing me. Elysia, just do it and let's go. What?

Raven turned and saw Elysia reciting a spell. Raven shouted her name, but she just smirked as she finished the spell. Suddenly, Raven found herself unconscious yet aware of her surroundings. It was as if someone possessed her and was controlling her movements. She could do nothing, yet she saw everything. She couldn't speak but she could hear herself in her head.

Raven screamed yet no one heard. Instead of her normal, quirky demeanor, Elysia appeared without emotion. Almost as if her soul had been ripped from her body. Elysia somehow read her thoughts. She shook her head. My soul is still intact, sister. I have just found a new way of understanding. Soon you will feel the same.

NOOO!!!!!!

*****

Raven awoke, and it took a moment to realize she was still chained in the Sacian dungeon.

A guard asked, "Bad dream, bounty hunter?"

"Something like that." She tested the chains once more. There was no getting out of these. Cameron made damn sure she wouldn't be going anywhere. She was shaken because of the realness of the dream, but the reality of her situation pushed the dream to the back of her mind. "I don't suppose I can get a drink of water."

"What are you worried about water for?" One guard laughed. "You'll be dead tomorrow, anyway."

"Just as well. I hear there's some kind of darkness coming, and I sure don't want to be around for that."

The guards laughed again. "The only darkness coming is the one the elves will see. We're going to wipe the vermin from this realm and claim their lands and their wealth for our own!"

"Sounds ambitious. Are you sure your new king is up to it?"

The guard slammed his hand against the bars of her cell. "You just watch your mouth, girl! How dare you speak of the king in that tone! He wants you alive, but that doesn't mean I can't rough you up some."

"Oooh, you sure you can handle it?"

"That's enough."

The guard spun around and saw King Cameron coming down the steps leading into the dungeon. He bowed and apologized to his king.

"That's alright. Raven speaks without regard for whom she's speaking to or about."

"Oh, I know a snake when I see one."

"Charming as always, bounty hunter. I would just kill you now, but I need to make an example of you. I will show all of Sacia that you aided the escape of a wanted murderer. A murderer who returned to assassinate our beloved king. I'm sure you will not be well received, and the people will beg me to kill you. After that, I will declare war on the elves and finish what Warrick should have. Instead, the spineless coward befriended the same ones who killed his own wife."

"You are the coward, Cameron. I know for a fact the elf you speak of was wrongly accused. You had no intention of letting King Warrick near him. He would have been dead and so would I. There was no way you would have let me walk away from that meeting."

"Believe as you wish, bounty hunter. I remember that scenario differently. You and that elf attacked me and my guards, and then escaped from the castle. All I wanted was to escort the prisoner to King Warrick myself."

"That is a lie, and you know it. You will get what is coming to you, LORD Cameron!"

Cameron glared at her for a moment, but then returned to his calm demeanor. "I look forward to your execution tomorrow. There is no one left to save you."

"Perhaps, but who says I need anyone to save me."

"Dear, dear Raven. After tonight, you will beg me to kill you tomorrow. No one makes a fool of me."

"And just what do you plan to do? Torture me?"

"I don't plan to do anything. However, I won't be around if someone comes to pay you a visit."

"I swear I will kill you myself, traitor!"

"You really shouldn't swear, my dear. I hear it can be bad for your health."

Raven spit at him and the guard opened the cell door and punched her in the gut. She groaned but locked eyes on Cameron. She cursed him and the guard hit her in the face.

"I grow bored with you, Raven. I would say goodnight, but I fear it will be anything but. Guard, I will leave one of my personal guards to rotate with you tonight. I want to keep an eye on her at all times, understand?"

"Yes, your Majesty." The guard bowed again and then turned and glowered at Raven.

"You and I are gonna have some fun."

Raven sneered at the guard. "You have no idea."

*****

A couple of hours had passed, and Raven was tiring. She was extremely uncomfortable and bleeding from her restraints. What passed for food was scraps left over from the day's meal. They had dropped it on the floor, and she knew they did this on purpose. She looked around for any chance to escape, but again found nothing to give her hope.

Raven heard the door to the dungeon open, and a man entered from the shadow of the hallway. He was older and his head was balding. His nose was crooked, probably broken more than once. The man had scars on his face, and she assumed more across his body. He wasn't necessarily muscular, but from his expression, he knew how to torture people. Without him even speaking, she knew why he was there. She also had an idea who he was. She had heard stories of him through her travels. He carried a satchel which no doubt contained the tools he would use on her. As fierce as Raven was, she knew she was about to experience pain unlike anything she had felt in her lifetime. She knew also that he would still leave her alive for tomorrow's execution.

Fear. For the first time in a long time, she felt genuine fear. All that toughness she had built up in order to survive on her own was melting away. The guard opened the cell, and the man stepped inside. He smiled at Raven, but there was no joy in it. Well, no joy that was intended for Raven.

The man finally spoke. "Ahh, Lady Raven. My name is Stren. I've heard so much about you. Any other time, it would fascinate me to hear stories of your life. Tonight, however, I merely mean to break you. I want to hear your screams. I want you to beg me to stop, but I promise I won't until I decide it is time to stop."

"Stren, was it?" Raven struggled to maintain any composure. "Why don't you just let me go? Cameron has gone mad with power, and he must be stopped. Surely you can see that."

"None of that matters to me. Much like you, I stay out of the politics of kingdoms, and simply do what I'm paid to do. You, of all people, must understand that. All those bounties you gained over the years. Did you not enjoy doing that? The thrill of the hunt. The satisfaction of completing your contract, whether your victims were dead or alive. You should appreciate what I do. Since it is now your turn to be the victim, are you going to reject your destiny? This could be your penance for all of those lives you have taken. It truly is a bit ironic. How many of your bounties pleaded for you to let them go? Then, the one time you gave in and let a bounty go, you wound up here with me. It's almost poetic if you think about it."

"What I did and what you do are completely different. The only deaths on my hand were in self-defense. I murdered no one, contrary to what's been said of me. They pay you to torture and kill. I have heard of you as well, Stren."

"Enough of the pleasantries then. I shall get to work. Don't worry. I will start out easy on you. I have all night to play."

Stren pulled out a whip with barb tips on the end. Raven winced and struggled in vain against her restraints, but he simply smiled at her. There was some truth to what he said, and it hit her like a rock. She enjoyed the hunt, and the killing had become easier to where she no longer hesitated, nor thought much about it afterward. Just another bounty. Perhaps this was her punishment. Either way, she tried to brace herself for what was coming. Raven had no idea how much it was going to hurt.

Chapter Twenty-Three

Liam, Evan, and Theron ran as fast and as far as they could go before stopping to rest. They were all still weakened from their injuries. While healed, their muscles still felt wobbly. They knew they were in a race against time. Liam knew they were still about three days until they reached the Paelean border. They had started out on the road to Paelea but found Cameron had patrols out looking for Liam and Evan. They took trails that were considered shortcuts, but it was through the thickest parts of the forest. That alone would slow their pace, but by doing so, they hoped they wouldn't be tracked. After a while, they were slowed to a walk as their energy was draining and the forest was more difficult to traverse. They stopped another time to eat a little of their rations. They ate very little at a time, knowing their food had to last at least a couple more days. If nothing else, perhaps they would run into a Paelean patrol, and they would be brought before the king, if they weren't killed on-sight.

At one of their stops, Liam wondered about Raven. He wanted to see if she was in trouble, as Elysia had said, but knew that would be a suicide mission. He hoped she was as tough as she made herself out to be. She was going in with no one to watch her back. He had Evan, but still, they almost didn't make it. Shouldn't have made it. They were lucky Elysia showed up when she did. He had to give her credit. She could have left them for dead, but she didn't. Because of that, he trusted her to an extent. He knew she wanted a favor from them for healing them, but he would deal with that later. They had to reach Paelea before King Rhys set out to attack, not knowing Warrick's son was still alive.

Liam's mind quickly returned to his surroundings when he heard rustling to the west. Someone or something was out there. They each hid behind trees and waited as the rustling sound came closer to where they were. Suddenly, an arrow struck the tree right above Liam's head. This came from behind them.

"It's an ambush!" Liam yelled. They were so busy listening to what appeared to be coming at them, they missed the archers lining up behind them. Somehow, they had been found. They scurried even deeper into the forest as arrows either sailed over them or stuck in the trees surrounding them. They didn't know how many there were, but they really didn't want to find out. Even in their tired state, they were still quicker than their attackers, as they were probably wearing armor. Eventually, they came across a ravine and all three dove into it. Evan peered over and counted six soldiers coming toward them, but he could tell they didn't know exactly where they were. He whispered to Liam and Evan that they might have a chance if they could sneak around them. Liam agreed, but Theron stopped them.

"I'm not trained for this. I'm not sure how much help I'll be."

Liam placed a hand on his shoulder.

"You'll be fine. Just follow our lead. As we make our way around quietly, try to find something that can be used as a weapon. If we can take out a couple of them, then we can take their swords. Evan, you go first. You are a better tracker and would know the best way to get us behind them."

Evan nodded and motioned for them to head south along the ravine. After several yards, they snuck around and silently followed the soldiers. Along the way, they both picked up limbs from the ground large enough to work as makeshift weapons. Once they got close to the soldiers, Liam pointed to the two nearest ones and Evan nodded. Liam calmly walked up to the soldiers and asked if they were lost. The soldiers spun around, but it was too late as Liam and Evan slammed the limbs across their helmets. This staggered the soldiers and before they could recover, the prince and his bodyguard grabbed their swords and stabbed their assailants. Liam stared down at the man he had just killed, knowing he was one of his own countrymen. He didn't see the archer level an arrow at him, but the arrow whizzed wildly to his left. Liam looked up and saw Theron standing over the soldier with a tree limb of his own. He picked up the bow and the quiver of arrows and ran behind a tree. By that time, the three remaining soldiers were on top of them, and Liam and Evan did their best to hold them off. They were tired and losing ground when one soldier fell. Evan took a quick peek and saw Theron line up the next one. He ducked and Theron dropped the soldier with a shot in his neck. He then felled the last one engaged with Liam. Theron let out a whoop, but there was no celebration by Liam. Evan patted his friend on the back.

"These men were not your countrymen. They knew who you were and still attacked. These men are traitors, period."

"I know. Still, I can't believe it. What has happened to Sacia? Did Cameron really turn this many against my father? If we somehow succeed in removing Cameron from the throne, how can I trust anyone to be loyal?"

"You can figure that out when the time comes. We need to keep moving. Who knows how many more groups like this are tracking us."

"Liam held up the sword he took from a soldier. At least now we're not defenseless. Gather what we can and let's go."

Liam walked up to Theron and punched him lightly in the chest.

"You're the hero today, Theron. I didn't know you could use a bow like that."

"I didn't know if I could. I've practiced a lot with a bow, but only against stationary targets. This is the first time against targets that actually fought back."

"Well, you have proven yourself today. Come on, let's move."

"I need to say something first."

Liam and Evan looked back at their friend.

"The reason I admired Lord Cameron was because of his hatred of elves. I guess I've always heard the horrible stories about them and took the stories at face value. After I was almost killed, and hearing the truth about Raven and her prisoner, I know I was lied to. I will keep an open mind now. I promise you both can trust me."

Liam put his hand on Theron's shoulder. "If I thought any differently, Theron, you would not have come with us. From this point on, we all have new beginnings. I trust you with my life."

"Thank you, Prince Liam. I won't let you down."

"I know you won't, and just call me Liam. You've more than earned that."

Chapter Twenty-Four

King Cameron made his way from the dungeon up to his throne room. He sat on the throne and rubbed the arms of the chair with his hands, soaking up the reality that he was now king. Everything was going to plan except the part about Prince Liam. His nephew was missing but presumed dead by his guards. However, his body had not been discovered, and if there was no body, he had to assume Liam was still alive.

Cameron had soldiers scouring the countryside for them. As badly hurt as they were, they shouldn't be this hard to find. Each report that returned to him, though, was the same as the one before. They found no Liam or Evan. They discovered blood in the woods close to the castle walls, but no trails were left from there. It was as if they had vanished. Cameron knew better than that. They were out there somewhere, and he hoped they were dead. If Liam showed up, the people might demand the prince be crowned king, and Cameron removed and executed. He wouldn't have any of that. Raven had tried to sneak in and failed. Tomorrow, she would be executed, and should they find Liam alive, he ordered his soldiers to kill him onsight and bury the body where it could not be found.

Cameron looked out at his chamber. Only he and a couple of guards were in the room. They stood at the only known door to the throne room. He knew there was a second door the king could slip through should trouble start for whatever reason. It was directly behind the throne, hidden from view by a dark blue tapestry that bore the Sacian crest in gold. Once inside, he could seal the door and make his way through a tunnel to the other side of the castle.

Tunnel. Of course! That's how Liam escaped! He remembered now that his nephew used to disappear and would be found outside of the castle walls. That's how he did it!

Cameron called his guards and ordered them to search the castle for any trap doors or false walls. He wanted as many of these tunnels found before Liam, should he still be alive, to make any attempt to re-enter the castle. He cursed aloud as if he should have remembered this sooner. Cameron might have caught them escaping and he wouldn't have this loose end dangling. A dangerous loose end at that.

Cameron wished it had not come to this. For years he tried to convince Liam how evil the Elven people were, but he was too much like his father. He could not understand why they did not hate the elves as much as he did. Even after they had, in his eyes, murdered Warrick's wife, his sister. That had only fueled his hatred. That aside, he despised them for being different. Different in beliefs and in appearance. He hated them for merely existing. He also felt Sacia was the rightful owner of the Paelean lands and that they were invaders that would never leave.

Millennia before, Sacia owned most of the land in this part of the realm. Due to war and a legend of a dragon attack, Sacia was divided. Most of the new kingdoms that arose were human, but one kingdom that emerged on conquered Sacian land was Paelea. An Elven tribe that had been exiled from their homeland because of conflicts with their Elven king found a home on land no one at the time wanted. Scorched and in ruins, the humans gave the land to the nomad elves. They healed the land and turned it into one of the richest regions in the realm.

As the prosperity of the elves soared, the other kingdoms became jealous. Over time, everyone relented and officially recognized the newer Elven kingdom as legitimate. Everyone, that is, except Sacia. King after king tried to either purchase or force the land from the elves. Each time, they refused to sell and fended off each attack. The Elven people were excellent warriors with fierce determination. However, the latest war truly tested the strength of the elves. They were faltering when Warrick emerged as king because of the passing of his father. His ceasefire gave the Elven people hope of a true and lasting peace. Now, war was once again inevitable. Warrick was gone and Liam was presumed dead, and the new king aimed to finish what Warrick's father had started.

King Cameron loved his nephew, but Liam stood in the way of what he envisioned Sacia could be. It saddened him to order his death, but knew it was necessary to restore glory to his kingdom.

His kingdom. He loved the sound of that. Cameron gave himself another moment to soak in the fact he was king now. He would let no one take that away from him. The incident with the bounty hunter forced his hand to hasten, but he decided Raven did him a favor. By performing her "noble" act, Raven kept him from overthinking his plans, or worse yet, backing out altogether. He was second guessing himself, but once Raven escaped, the decision was made for him. He reminded himself to thank Raven before her death. Now he had to ensure his nephew was also dead so that nothing or no one could get in his way.

Regarding his plan of attack, he signed new recruits every day. Cameron promised anyone who joined, their families would be taken care of while they were away. He pushed his officers to order the soldiers on leave to return, and to get the new recruits as much training as possible in a short amount of time. He hated having such an inexperienced army, but his plans for the recruits were that they were expendable, anyway. Cameron had instructed his officers to put them on the front lines to absorb most of the enemy's fire once they charged on Paelea. This would leave his more experienced soldiers to deal with the Elven soldiers once they breached their castle walls and gate.

He also sent word to other kingdoms in the realm. Cameron would reward anyone who joined once Paelea fell. He promised riches he hoped couldn't be turned down.

Sacia would win, Cameron decided. He felt he was destined to do this. Everything was lining up perfectly and Paelea would not deny him his victory. His entire scheme was to strengthen Sacia but inside, he knew his name would be etched in history as well. This thought brought a smile to Cameron's face. He would be the Sacian king who reclaimed some of their ancient lands and rid the realm of an inferior race. Yes, he would be that king, indeed.

Chapter Twenty-Five

Elysia awoke from her healing sleep in a cold sweat. Mother was summoning her. How could mother summon her when she was dead? At first she dismissed it as a dream. A dream her magic conjured up while she rested. There was one problem. She could still hear the summons in her head, and she was awake now.

Coming out of a healing sleep left her groggy for several minutes, and she was still getting her senses about her. She tossed a couple of logs in her stove to heat some tea. This always helped ease her way back to her normal self. Well, normal for her. She led anything but a normal life. Raven called her mad and a witch. Perhaps there was a bit of truth to that. She had lived out here on her own about half her life. She enjoyed the company of others, but if anyone had ever suspected she possessed and used magic, she might be imprisoned and/or killed for it.

Elysia didn't understand regular humans, anyway. She understood their fear of magic, though. She had been fearful of it herself when she first discovered her magic. Elysia thought she was possessed, or something of that nature. She was ten and sat by a stream on a beautiful, sunny day. As she watched a few tadpoles twitching back and forth at the edge of the water, she looked up and saw a wild boar watching her. At first, the boar only took a couple of steps slowly in her direction, but when she stood up, the boar started running toward her. She took off running, but the boar was catching up. She realized she couldn't get away, so she turned and braced herself for her inevitable death. Suddenly, purple lightning sprung from her hands and dropped the boar. Its momentum caused the boar to slide right up to where she was and stopped, just a few inches from her. She just stared at her hands, and then at the boar, and trembled in fear. That moment was forever etched into her memory. She was never the same after that.

She simply avoided people now as much as possible and made a home from an old, abandoned shack deep in the forest. A home that had seen no one outside of the sorcerer for years, until now. Now, she had allowed three strangers to roam about as she slept. Had she not known one of them was the prince of Sacia, she probably wouldn't have. Her survival depended on her staying secluded.

Elysia, come to me, my child.

"No! Whoever you are, you lie! My mother's dead! Just leave me be!"

No, not dead. I need you to find me. Find me and help me.

"I will do no such thing!"

Please, my child. I need you to find me before the beast does. You can prevent what's coming if you help me.

Elysia was shaken. The voice knew what she knew. Was the voice simply in her head? Or…

No, it couldn't be! She was told her mother had died giving birth to her. "How do you know what's coming?" Silence answered her. She searched her house, but no one was there. Perhaps she was going mad.

Do not fear me, child. I mean you no harm, but you must hurry. I don't think I can hide from the beast much longer.

"Where are you? How am I to find you if I know nothing of your whereabouts?"

Just head north, beyond Sacia. I will guide you from there.

"Beyond Sacia? Now I know I am going mad. There are people here that need my help! I'm not going there."

Elysia purposely left Raven's name out. She wasn't sure if this was some reincarnation of her mom or some evil force trying to gather up those who had magic. Either way, she wasn't putting Raven at any more risk. Besides, if it truly was her mother, she would know of Raven already.

You must come, daughter. The fate of the realm and beyond depends on your decision at this moment. You are powerful. More so than you even know. I have sensed Raven has unlocked hers as well but is at a dangerous point in her life. Her lack of control over her magic prevents me from reaching her.

Elysia froze in place at hearing Raven's name. She knew about her! Could this be her mother? Her mind raced at the thought of her mother being alive. At least she thought she was alive.

"You know of my sister, then? Now you know why I can't leave. I must teach her to control her magic if she'll let me."

Raven will not let you help, daughter. She was always strong-willed to the point of being stubborn. She will resent you should you keep pushing her. Now, will you come?

Elysia let out a sigh. Regardless of whether this was her mother, she was right. Raven would continue to push her away. As much as she wanted to stay and help her, she knew Raven did not want her advice at all. She gave in and told the voice she would make the trip after all. She hoped if this was in fact a trick, her magic would help her escape. Elysia gathered a small knapsack of essentials, stepped outside, and saw Raven's horse standing nearby, eating grass at the edge of the woods. She ran up and grabbed the note attached. Worry filled her mind, but Raven would not want her meddling again. At least her sister trusted her enough to leave her horse with her for safekeeping. Elysia grabbed Shadow by her reins and gently led her to a small corral behind the house. It was in a state of disrepair but should hold her until Raven returned. There was plenty of grass and the creek ran just to the edge of the fence so she would have plenty of water.

Elysia started down the pathway and began her long journey to wherever it was she was going. She had no horse and didn't dare take Raven's, but she preferred walking anyway. It helped her stay close to nature. Nature seemed to fuel her magic, and so she went. As she walked through the thick of the forest, she turned back to look at her home one last time. She wondered if she would ever see it again.

She spun toward Sacia. "Raven!"

She could sense her magic. Raven was losing control. Mother would have to wait. Elysia took off, running toward the dangerous energy she was feeling. If Raven made it out of the castle, it was possible she might head for the lake. Fire was fire, even if created by magic. Raven would head there.

Elysia finally made it to the shore of the lake on the west side of the castle. Now she waited to see if her instincts were right.

*****

Raven steeled herself as the barbed tip of Stren's whip ripped open the skin on her back. Tears fell from her eyes, but she refused to scream. She wanted to, but held it in. She would not give Stren the satisfaction. The more he lashed at her, though, the angrier it made her. If she could somehow break free, she would kill them all. She knew that was probably not going to happen. By the time Stren was finished, she would not be able to move, much less fight back.

Stren stopped for a moment and admired the blood streaming down her back. He could see the sweat and tears rolling off Raven's face, but she held it together enough to glare at him.

"Stop trying to be so brave, bounty hunter. I'm just getting started. We have all night to play."

"Then let's play fair," Raven said, almost whispering. "Untie me and see how much fun we'll have."

"I see you still have your humor intact. That will be the first to go, I assure you. Shall we continue?"

"Do your worst, coward."

"Oh, believe me, bounty hunter. I plan to. King Cameron paid extra for my finest work. I don't plan to disappoint."

Raven groaned as she dropped her head. She was already exhausted and hurting. Stren continued lashing at her. Her anger returned. With each strike, she felt anger building up inside. She glanced down at her hands, and she saw smoke forming in her palms. Raven closed her eyes as if not believing what she saw. She opened her eyes again and sure enough, smoke was emanating from them and growing thicker. Stren also noticed and stopped. He gazed at her, and his eyes widened.

"The king didn't say you were a witch. That's gonna cost him extra."

Raven shook her head. *No, no, no,* she thought. She remembered Elysia telling her she wouldn't be able to control it. Raven remembered the story of the sorcerer Elysia knew, and how he died losing control of his power. She tried to suppress her anger, but it was no use. Her hands glowed a fiery red, and she watched as they burst into flames so hot, the shackles on her arms melted almost immediately. Stren stepped back to where his satchel lay and retrieved a dagger from it. The situation had changed and now he must kill her before she freed herself completely. He charged at her with the dagger, and she reached out her hand to stop him. A small fireball erupted from her outstretched hand and caught Stren right in the gut. His clothes burst into flames, and he started screaming. She reached down and grabbed the shackles on her ankles, and those melted away as well.

The guards standing outside of her cell stood there in shock as Cameron's personal guard ran up the steps to warn the others. The guard closest to the cell door stood with his sword extended, not sure that he could do any good. He knew letting Raven escape would be death for him anyway, so he stood his ground. Raven sneered at him through the bars and demanded he unlock the cell door. The guard refused. At this point, the flames surrounding her hand turned blue. She reached for the bars, and they melted away. The guard tried to stab her through the cell door. She grabbed the end of it and the sword melted clear down to the handle. Raven stepped through where the bars had melted away and the guard pulled out a dagger and threw it at her. It landed in her chest, just above her heart. Raven stepped back for a second and winced. She pulled out the dagger, and it dropped into a ball of molten steel. She glared at the guard and then sent him flying with another fireball.

That one hurt. She looked down at her hands, and they were blue and white. The flames were getting way too hot! She could not control her magic and was feeling the heat through her arms. She had to get out of the palace, and quickly. There was a lake on the other side of the castle, and she had to reach it before she exploded or erupted into flames.

She made it up to the door and ignited the wood immediately. She kicked through the door at the hinges and the wood splintered and slammed into a couple of guards on the other side. Others came rushing toward her, but she spread flames from her that doused several soldiers and sent more running for cover. She groaned in anguish at this point and felt her entire body temperature rise. Her arms ached terribly, and she was running out of time. She ran down the hallway and disposed of anyone who got in her way.

Raven made her way out of the castle and into the courtyard. She ran for the gate and found the archers had scrambled up on top of the walls around her and rained down arrows in her direction. One grazed her shoulder, but she didn't stop. Her muscles ached from being shackled and stretched out, but she paid them no mind.

Can't stop now! She told herself. Raven reached the gate and threatened the guards. The flames increased around her hands as she was making a large fireball. The guards just looked at each other and opened the gate. Raven ran through the crack as soon as it was wide enough and ran into the woods. She didn't look back but could see arrows shooting past her. She was in severe pain now. Her arms burned, and she struggled to maintain her balance. Why didn't she just listen to Elysia? Her own stubbornness was going to kill her this time. Raven continued running and almost stumbled twice. She knew if she fell, she probably could not get back up. She pushed on and soon she saw a clearing ahead of her.

The lake! Raven had reached the lake. She ran even harder, and her body was really getting hot. She made it to the clearing and several yards away were the blue-green waters of the lake. Raven leaped over a couple of dead trees that had long fallen over and reached the shoreline. She dove in and began swimming. Every muscle felt like they were going to tear loose, but she had to reach the other side of the lake. She would allow herself a few moments to rest but knew they would be after her. Several minutes later, she reached the far shore and fell into the water and swam. Barely keeping herself above water, she found her way back to shore farther down the lake and collapsed at the edge of the water. She looked down at her arms and they were burned up to her elbows. The flames had extinguished finally, but she lay on the beach in severe pain. Raven crawled toward the woods to at least get herself out of sight. She almost made it but found herself too weak to continue. She collapsed on the edge of the beach, but before she blacked out, she thought she saw someone approach. Darkness engulfed her, leaving her to wonder if she had died.

Chapter Twenty-Six

King Cameron heard a knock on the door of his study. He had asked to be left alone unless something needed his urgent attention. He was curious about what prompted this intrusion so late in the evening.

"Come in," Cameron ordered.

The guard he had left to help watch Raven was standing in the doorway.

"What happened? Why are you not watching over Raven?"

The guard bowed. "Sire, Raven is gone!"

Cameron stood and clenched his fists. "What?!? How could this possibly have happened? She was chained inside the cell!"

"She… She has powers, milord."

"What do you mean, she has powers? I have never heard of such things with her. Magic disappeared from this realm decades ago!"

"She has them, your Majesty. She used fire to melt her chains off and then used it to escape. We tried to stop her, but she was too powerful!"

"What of Stren? Where is he?"

"Dead, sire."

Cameron's anger flared. First Liam and now Raven.

"Are you all so incompetent that you couldn't stop her?"

"Sire, several dozen are dead or with serious burns. We tried!"

"And failed!" Cameron nodded to his guards and one of them pulled his sword and stabbed the guard in his back.

The guard was shocked as he looked down and saw the sword protruding out of his body. He grabbed the blade as blood poured out and dropped to his knees.

"Forgive me, sire…," were his last words.

The guard pulled the sword out and sheathed it. The king looked down at the man and shook his head.

"I don't forgive failure."

The king walked into the dungeon where his men lay dead. Several were burned to a crisp and in the cell lay Stren, or what was left of him. His body lay blackened and unrecognizable. He never knew she had such powers. She had never shown them before, nor had he heard rumors of her magic. Cameron walked out into the courtyard where the guards at the gate saw him and snapped to attention.

Once again, this bounty hunter was forcing his hand. He ordered a small battalion to look for her. He made sure he sent several of his finest archers along with them. Once they found her, they would need to attack from a distance to avoid her magic. Now he would have to order a strike on Paelea. He couldn't afford for Raven to return to stop him. Several of his men said she looked like she was in pain as she fled the castle. If this was true, it bought him some time. However, he did not want to risk her coming back to foil his plans, so he would need to round up all the soldiers to plan the attack. He ordered all his commanders to his meeting room to discuss the plan of attack. Cameron demanded the full army to be gathered at once. He sent riders to Sleston since it was the closest kingdom to see if they would send a regiment to aid in their plans. War was again coming to the realm. Cameron looked out once more over the courtyard. He hoped the ones he sent out would be fortunate enough to take care of the bounty hunter. If not, he would have to deal with her at another time. Now it was time to gather his forces and head for Paelea.

Chapter Twenty-Seven

"I swear, I cannot leave any of you alone without someone getting hurt."

Raven opened her eyes and saw Elysia standing by her. She looked around and noticed she was in bed back at Elysia's home. She was groggy, in pain, and in no mood for her antics. Raven just rolled over and turned her back to Elysia.

"Oh, just kill me now."

"Now, now. Is that any way to treat the person who just saved your life?"

Raven noticed the linen wraps on her arms. Her arms hurt, but they weren't as bad as before. She felt something on her back as well. It was obvious Elysia knew Raven had gotten in way over her head.

"How did you find me?"

Elysia smiled and shook her head.

"I felt your energy, and I could feel it escalating and knew you were going to spiral out of control. I guessed you might head to the lake… if you made it at all."

Raven rolled back over, only to see an eyebrow arched at her.

"Don't you dare say it."

"I tried to warn you."

Raven sighed.

"So, where are the boys?" Hoping to change the subject.

"They were gone when I woke up. Since I found no more bodies, I would assume they headed for Paelea."

Raven rolled on to her back. She struggled to get comfortable. She missed her old life where she was alone and didn't have to deal with — well, Elysia.

Elysia continued. "This friendly couple passing through gave us a ride."

"What?" *Where did this come from?* Raven wondered.

"You didn't use your magic?"

"I still haven't fully recovered from healing your friends."

"They're not my… wait… You led them here? What about your secrecy?"

Elysia waved her hand at her. "No, no. I just told them to drop us by the woods near the house. I said your husband would come and get you from here. They asked about your wounds. I told them we had been to the tavern, and that you had drank way too much. We made camp by the lake before heading back the next day. Your wounds, I told them, were from you tripping and landing hands first in the fire."

"My husband? They bought that story?"

Elysia just laughed. "Yeah, I told them your husband would be angry with us, and that it would be best to drop us off here."

Raven had to admit it wasn't a completely horrible story, and it obviously worked. They were here, alright.

"So, how did you make out? I take it Cameron is still alive?"

Raven remembered getting caught, being tortured, and almost burning herself alive.

"Yeah, that didn't turn out quite like I had hoped."

"Well sweetie, sometimes you have to learn the hard way."

Raven sneered at her but said nothing. She hated that her alleged sister was right, but she had been right about everything. Raven explained getting caught and spending the evening being tortured. She recalled the more he hit her, the angrier she became until her hands ignited. At first, she felt like she had control of her power, but soon found out she did not. She escaped, but every time she used her magic, the more she hurt. The last thing she remembered before collapsing was seeing someone walk up and figured she was dead.

Elysia lowered herself so that she was kneeling and looked Raven in the eyes with a serious enough expression that it startled her.

"That was me. You are lucky you thought to head for the lake. The water itself isn't enough to squelch the fire, but your concentration on swimming, plus your exhaustion, helped to calm the magic inside you. I know you think of me as just some crazy witch. Perhaps I am a bit quirky, but if you do not listen to me, sister, the next time, you might not be so lucky. You must learn to control your magic. If not, it will consume and destroy you, as you certainly found out."

Raven was speechless. She knew now she needed help with her…

problem. She hated having to depend on other people, especially someone claiming to be her sister. Raven still couldn't wrap her head around that. She knew she had no other option. She had to swallow her pride to say what she was about to say.

"I realize my… condition… is a problem for me. I know my anger fuels a lot of it."

Raven sighed and fought herself to say what she needed to say next.

"Will you help me control it?"

Elysia smiled. "First, it's not a condition, it's a gift."

"Forgive me if I don't see it as such."

"I will help you…"

Raven knew it. She wanted to take it all back now. She knew there would be a 'but.' "But you need something in return, right?"

Elysia shrugged her shoulders and looked off as if staring at something that only she could see.

"While you were off trying to kill yourself, I had something happen to me."

"Let me guess, you had a vision of the future, of this darkness you keep mentioning."

"Not exactly a vision. More like a voice that reached out to me."

So, she is losing her mind, Raven thought, but played along.

"And just what did this voice tell you? To go find this beast you have spoken of before?"

"No, well, not really. It involves the dragon, though."

"Please, tell me more."

"You won't believe me."

"You seem surprised by this."

Elysia waved her hand in dismissal.

"Our mother is alive, sort of."

"Our mother? You think you heard a voice, and that voice was our mother? I'm trying hard to give you the benefit of the doubt, but you keep throwing things at me that make me think that you truly are crazy."

"I'm not crazy!" Elysia snapped. Her eyes glowed purple, and she leaned down, placing her hands on the side of the bed. "Maybe I've been playing like I've been a little off this whole time to throw you off! Perhaps I just wanted you to think I was some harmless trickster. Maybe I killed your friends and buried them out back!"

The sudden mood change took aback Raven. She's seen it before, but not to this extreme.

"Did you kill them?"

Elysia rolled her eyes and shook her head.

"No, Raven, I didn't. I told you, they are probably on their way to speak to King Rhys. We can go find them, but we'll be going way out of the way."

"Calm down. You are all over the place, so I don't know what to believe. Just where are you going?"

"I must see for myself if that is truly our mother and I need you to go with me. She doesn't think you will."

Raven was quiet for a moment. Talking to this woman gave her a serious headache.

"You realize it's probably some sort of trap. Let's just say for a moment we're sisters. I still don't buy it, but never mind that for now. You think our mother spoke to you, not in a dream, but while you were wide awake? Have I got this right so far?"

Elysia nodded.

"Okay. She told you she's not awake, but will be, and that a dragon is coming for her. Do you hear how crazy this sounds?"

Elysia shrugged. "You thought that you having magic was crazy as well, but I guess I can see where this might be confusing."

Raven looked down at her arms and conceded her point.

"Everything about what's happened lately is confusing. Magic was something of legends, and I wondered if it was all fairy tales to gloss over what might have really happened. Now, I realize I have been wrong about a lot of things. Regardless, I will go with you, if you will stay and help us defeat Cameron. I swear I will then accompany you on this journey you feel you must take. Did Shadow return to you by chance?"

Elysia smiled and told her Shadow was behind the house. However, whatever was happening, the time to leave was now. She had already delayed her trip, but she couldn't have left Raven to die. Elysia knew that because they were sisters, they both were tied to what lay ahead. She explained to Raven that she should go with her now. Elysia could help her control her powers as they headed north. She warned Raven should she stay and fight, she could lose control again and she might be worse off than she is now. Besides, they fought wars without her in the past. If they couldn't stop what was coming, the result would be meaningless, no matter who won.

Raven looked at her arms again, bandages wrapped to her shoulders. She had to admit that she wouldn't be able to fight for a while. She couldn't even feed or dress herself. That frustrated her to no end. The thought of traveling with Elysia made her head spin, but she knew the woman was right. She wanted to see this person who claimed to be their mother. Raven finally relented. The war would be left to Liam and the elves to win. Her vengeance toward Cameron would have to be shelved, at least for now.

"Fine. I will accompany you to wherever it is you're going. I can't fight or do anything in my condition, anyway. If we're discovered before we leave Sacia, I'm afraid I won't be much help."

"Leave that to me. I have a knack for being invisible."

"Unless I'm around."

Elysia smiled. She wasn't about to tell Raven that she had been watching her for years. She had only approached her recently for reasons she had already revealed. However, Elysia saw no reason to tell her this right now. Maybe later. Maybe.

Chapter Twenty-Eight

Liam, Evan, and Theron avoided any more search parties. They came across a scout and allowed him to get close enough to be captured by Evan and Theron. Now they had a prisoner, which slowed them down even more. They looked ahead and knew they had to be close to the Paelean border. War destroyed the land on both sides of the border, leaving few settlements. Those that did, had long been abandoned.

Evan approached the clearing and saw a small garrison looking into Paelea. They were definitely Sacian, which was going to make crossing into Paelea tricky. They knew if they came across the Paelean army, they could surrender to them and ask to speak with King Rhys. Also, they figured the Sacian army had orders to kill them on site. No way would Cameron risk having Liam brought back to the castle alive. He needed him and Evan dead. Liam came up to his friend's side with Theron right behind.

"I count twenty soldiers."

"Too many for you?" Evan countered.

"Today, yes. Elysia might have healed us, but my body still feels the effects of the last few days."

"You're just getting soft, old friend."

"And you're still annoying."

Evan chuckled. "Good to know I haven't lost my touch."

Theron looked out at the group of soldiers. "How are we going to get through them?"

"We wait," Liam replied. "Eventually, they will move on to another area and then hopefully, we can sneak past."

"We have to be careful, though." Evan chimed in. "They have several on horseback. If they see us, they would be on us, with the rest following not far behind."

Liam agreed. They didn't come all this way to get caught now. They had to be cautious. There were probably scouts scouring along the border looking for them. It was clear Cameron did not believe they were dead.

Theron was so focused on the army that lay ahead, he completely forgot he was holding the rope of their prisoner. The scout shoved Theron, and he fell to the ground, letting go of the rope.

The scout tried to scream, but he was still gagged so he ran as hard as he could through the clearing toward the army. Theron jumped back up and grabbed his bow as Liam and Evan realized what had just happened. Theron let go of an arrow and it pierced right through the scout's heart. He fell into the tall grass of the prairie. All three of them froze in place as several soldiers looked their way, not sure of what was going on. As a couple of men broke loose and headed toward them, they silently slipped further back into the woods and hoped the scout wouldn't be discovered. Liam and Evan unsheathed their swords, and Theron lined up his shot and waited.

Four soldiers branched out and looked to the edge of the forest, wading through knee high grass. One man walked dangerously close to the scout, but his eyes were focused ahead. One followed the tree line, peering in, but saw nothing. Another soldier ventured into the forest and looked around, but wasn't near where the three were hidden. The last one searched out along the prairie, where the grass thinned into the war-torn grounds near the border itself. The soldiers converged, and one of them just shrugged as they pointed in different directions. Finally, they headed back to the primary group and Liam let out a huge sigh. Theron lowered his bow and placed the arrow back into the quiver. Evan kept an eye focused on the soldiers as they all moved their attention west. Evan looked north and saw what appeared to be Paelean soldiers approaching. The Sacians could be heard cursing as the elves approached.

The two sides measured each other, but neither moved. Evan looked at Liam and pointed toward the standoff.

"I see them. This could be our chance. If we made a run for it, we might reach the border before they noticed us."

"It's wide open, so we would be sitting ducks if we're discovered," Evan countered.

"True, but we're wasting valuable time just hiding out here."

Theron spoke up. "I could help keep them at a distance if they see us. It might buy us a couple of minutes."

Liam thought for a moment. "Their archers are good. They would counter you tenfold.”

Liam paused. *Their archers.* Men who his father used to command were now his enemy. Thinking about that troubled him greatly.

Evan noticed his friend go silent and understood his conflict. “Cameron has them convinced what they’re doing is right. We know he’s not, which is why we must speak to King Rhys. We need his army to give you a chance to claim your place as the rightful heir to Sacia’s throne.”

“I know. It’s just hard to see these same men fight for the man who murdered my father. Some of them were even in on it.”

Liam looked back at the confrontation. The Sacians continued taunting the Elven army while they just stood in defiance. “This could get ugly.”

“Maybe not.” Evan watched the two armies and looked at his friends. “Now’s our chance. If we can make our way into Paelea and behind the two armies, we could surrender to Paelea here and now.”

“You know these men are not just going to let us go with Paelea. They need me dead.”

“Watch them closely. These men are not well-trained. They are erratic and have no structure other than the commander. Even he is agitating the Paelean army. Now look at the elves. They are organized and disciplined. If these men really want to attack the elves, they will be slaughtered. Either way, we’re in the clear… I hope.”

Liam studied the scene in front of him. Evan had a point. They could just wait it out, but there would be another regiment along soon. Probably more disciplined than these fools.

“I hate to admit this, but you’re right. Now is the time.”

“Did the mighty prince just admit his bodyguard might be smart?”

“Even a blind squirrel can find a nut.”

Theron laughed, and Evan just gave him a sarcastic stare. “I could send you back to the crazy witch if you like.”

Theron just smiled at his friend. “Hey, I don’t mind. She was easy on the eyes, plus she healed me. I’d be dead without her.”

Evan nodded in agreement. “I still don’t trust her, but at least we’re all alive, so I’ll give her a pass.” He looked over at Theron. “She was quite striking.”

Liam walked toward the edge of the trees. “While you two

lovesick puppies ogle over a witch, I am going to save my kingdom. Anyone care to join me?"

Evan cleared his throat. "Right behind you, my prince."

"Same here," replied Theron.

"Then let's go."

*****

Liam, Evan, and Theron snaked through the tall grass, careful not to draw attention their way. They made it about one hundred yards when the grass grew sparse and the battered grounds along the border spread out. Liam waved for them to stop and took a long look at the soldiers, preoccupied with their standoff with the Paelean regiment.

"I figure we can make it if we run. Hopefully, by the time they see us, we will be halfway to the border. Once there, keep running until the Paelean army orders us to stop. Then, we will surrender."

Evan nodded. "There really is no other way. We could try to sneak, but if they saw us, we wouldn't make it."

Liam looked back at Theron, and he nodded as well. He took another long look at the soldiers to the left of them. Finally, he took a deep breath and signaled for them to go. Liam started running, with Evan and Theron right behind him. They made it almost halfway to the Paelean border when he heard the Sacian soldiers yelling from a distance. He didn't even turn to look. Liam pushed himself harder and just focused ahead, careful not to trip on any stumps that might stick up from the ground. He could see arrows landing in front of them, which meant the archers had assembled and were approaching from the west.

They ran as hard as they could and when it seemed like they might not make it, the arrows suddenly stopped. Liam gave a quick glance and saw the Paelean army headed right for them. He slowed down enough to look back and heard the Sacian soldiers cursing at them. They wanted nothing more than to fight the Paeleans, but they were grossly outnumbered. Liam sighed. At least no more Sacian blood would be shed today.

As the Paelean soldiers approached, Liam could see their archers were ready to attack. Liam stopped and slowly unsheathed his sword and laid it gently on the ground in front of him. He then raised his arms in surrender, and Evan and Theron followed suit. The leader eased forward on his horse and glared at the three intruders.

"You dared try to sneak into Paelea while your fellow soldiers distracted us?"

Liam shook his head. "On the contrary, we were running from the soldiers. I am Liam Warrick, prince of Sacia and son of the late King Warrick. These are my friends, Evan and Theron. We wish to seek an audience with King Rhys. We surrender to you peacefully and request asylum."

Chapter Twenty-Nine

King Cameron stood at the window in his private chamber and watched the activity of the people below. Off in the distance, he saw the new recruits training. They were learning quickly but still needed time, something he didn't have. Raven had vanished. Liam and his bodyguard were missing. No one could find any of them. Either could ruin his plans. Cameron had to think of a backup strategy. He had several small bands of soldiers out looking for them. He couldn't take any chances with the new recruits. If they found out Liam was still alive, they might side with him. He would kill them, of course. He wasn't about to give up power now. His army was nearly ready for a full-on assault of Paelea. He had summoned every young boy as early as thirteen years of age to train for war. Most were eager to fight to avenge King Warrick while others were coerced to. Cameron learned that Sleston was supplying soldiers as well. He turned as he heard a knock at the door. "Enter."

An older man stepped in and bowed his head. "I have news, your Majesty."

"Good news, I hope. I grow tired of hearing failures to perform simple tasks."

The old man swallowed hard. "I-I'm afraid not, sire."

"What is it?"

"Some of our men were found dead and stripped of their weapons in the forest to the east."

King Cameron stood in silence, his rage returning. He knew this was Liam. He was alive and making his way toward Paelea.

Paelea. Liam was headed to the elves for asylum! This meant no surprise attack on the elves. Cameron cursed aloud and ordered the man to leave. He turned to Luther, who had accompanied the man. "I want all the commanders assembled at once! We can no longer wait. The time for our assault on the elves is at hand."

"Yes, your Majesty," Luther bowed and exited.

Cameron paced back and forth. He now hated the man he used to love as his own son. Except it wasn't his son. He had been taught to be weak by his own father. Now, he would pay for his treason. He mourned his death before, but now he *wanted* Liam dead.

"Why am I surrounded by fools?" Cameron yelled to no one. "Why can't anyone do anything right?"

Cameron stormed out of his chamber and headed for the meeting room. War was about to begin, and he planned to win it.

*****

The commanders were all gathered, and King Cameron looked among each one and scowled. "How soon can we be ready to move out?"

Top commander Girout spoke up. "We have the numbers, but many of them are still not ready."

"They'll have to be, commander. Place them in the front lines. They will help shield our more experienced men."

"But they'll be easily killed, milord."

"They will die with honor on the battlefield. Dare you question me a second time?"

The commander shook his head. "No, your Majesty."

"Good. I will ask once more and only once. How soon until we can leave?"

"We will be ready to move out in the morning, my king."

"Excellent! Soon, we will crush our enemy and reclaim the glory of Sacia! This will be a shining moment in our history!"

The commanders bowed in acknowledgment. Cameron dismissed them but asked Luther to stay. He asked about the loyalty of the commanders, particularly Girout.

"They all care about protecting Sacia."

Luther paused for a moment.

"If you don't mind me being blunt, my king, you are not as… open to questions as Warrick was. They just need to get used to your way of governing."

"From you, I expect bluntness, and I appreciate your candor. I will forgive him this time, but I want you to keep a close eye on Girout. If he cannot give me his full loyalty, I'll replace him."

"Yes, sire."

"One more thing. We cannot wait for Sleston's men to get here. Send a courier to them and have them go to Paelea directly. Have them attack their castle. They will more than likely be left with little protection. Paelea will not see this surprise coming."

Luther bowed and left the room. Cameron was angry at the recent failures of his soldiers. He questioned the competence of the Sacian army and put the blame solely on Warrick. They were as soft as he was. He had thought about postponing the attack, but Liam's escape left him no choice. If the people of Sacia knew he was still alive, he would have to deal with civil unrest. No, he had to proceed and be victorious to hold on to his power. If not, and civil unrest became a reality, well, he had plans for that as well. He hoped it would not come to that, but if it did, so be it. He would rule Sacia with an iron fist if he had to.

Chapter Thirty

Raven and Elysia traveled through the forest, staying off the main roads. Raven did not bring Shadow with them. She hurt too much to ride for one, but she didn't know how far they were going or what they were heading into. They both knew Sacia would look for not only Liam, but Raven as well. They figured they might run into a scouting party or two combing the woods for her, but Elysia had assured Raven, she could protect her. Protect her. Raven hated the thought of not being able to protect herself. She could tell the medicine Elysia had mixed was working, but she felt she was far from being able to use her hands and arms effectively. At least she was healing quickly. Had she been left on her own, she would be dead. Either by Cameron's men or her injuries. Whatever Elysia was using to speed up her healing, she was grateful for it.

Raven had expected Elysia to ramble on about whatever popped into her head, but she just walked, humming. Against her better judgment, she spoke up.

"Are you hearing the voice again?"

Elysia seemed to break from her trance. "It's hard to explain. I can hear her words, but it feels more like thoughts than sounds. She seems pleased you are joining me."

"She knows I'm with you?"

Elysia nodded.

"Ah, well, tell mother she won't be happy to see me if it is indeed her. I have a few bones to pick with her."

"Mother simply responded that you would understand in time."

"Good luck with that. I thought you were going to teach me how to control my powers. You have hardly said anything since we left."

"I wanted to see how long before you asked me this very question. I'm surprised at your patience."

"You mean this whole time you've been waiting for me to ask? Aren't we wasting time?"

"On the contrary, dear sister, patience is the key to controlling your magic. In your case, it seems to be tied to anger. Mine was fear. However, anger is much more dangerous. Mine appeared when I was being defensive and trying to protect myself. Your magic appeared when you became angry with me. I think when you escaped from Cameron with that elf, that must have unlocked your power somehow."

"And the patience part?"

"Yes, you need to be patient and calm, two things you seem to struggle with."

"I was plenty patient and calm until I met you."

"And obviously Cameron."

Raven rolled her eyes. "Well, that's for a different reason. You are maddening to talk to at times. I needed answers from you, and you would not answer me."

"Perhaps I was testing you. You aren't exactly someone who gets along with other people. If you had magic, I needed to know what you had. Your magic is powerful. Perhaps even more powerful than mine. I had to know before you found yourself in a situation…"

"You mean like this?" Raven held her hands up.

"Exactly. You are lucky that's the worst that happened."

"Well, it felt pretty bad at the time, but I know it could have been worse."

Raven stopped for a moment. The words she was about to say were something she wasn't used to, nor did she like saying it.

"Thank you for saving my life. I never expected to grow old living the life I've been leading, but I'm not ready to die just yet."

Elysia smiled. "Are you giving me a compliment?"

Raven shook her head. "Wait, no. I take it back. Never mind."

"Too late! I knew you would come around!"

Raven pointed her finger at Elysia. "I will leave right now and go to Paelea if you even think about hugging me."

"Fine! I'll behave… Maybe." The smile on Elysia's face didn't waver. She stopped walking and grabbed Raven by the arm.

"Don't! My arm!"

"Your arm should be better now."

Raven realized she felt no pain when Elysia grabbed it. "How did you know it wouldn't hurt?"

"I didn't, but I had a feeling you were to the point we could take these wrappings off." Elysia untied the knot to the bandages on

Raven's left arm and unrolled it carefully. Raven couldn't believe it. She could see the scars, but even those were faint.

"You did this? I mean, I know you healed the guys, but I thought I was scarred for life and completely useless for at least a few weeks. What you've done is…"

"Amazing?" Elysia grinned.

Raven smiled. "Yes, Elysia. Amazing."

She unwrapped her right arm and saw the same result. She turned her arms over and looked at them, still shocked that not only had they stopped hurting, but looked almost as good as new.

"Keep this up, and I will keep you around just to patch me up."

"Let's just hope I don't need to do this very often. You and your friends are quite clumsy, you know."

Raven shot her a look but said nothing. Elysia wasn't completely wrong, especially lately.

Chapter Thirty-One

Liam, Evan, and Theron walked between the regiment chained to each other as a precaution. Guards gave them water when requested, but ordered the men to remain silent otherwise. Once they arrived, the guards led them to an isolated room in the castle and stood outside to prevent them from escaping. A single window, tall and narrow, allowed them a view of the countryside. All three sat down on the stone floor to wait for whatever fate awaited them. Not long after, a guard entered the room, requesting them to stand as King Rhys approached. The king eyed all three of them as they stood at attention. It was obvious to Rhys the men were exhausted and probably hungry as well. First, he needed to know their true intentions.

"Which one of you claims to be Prince Liam Warrick of Sacia?"

Liam stepped forward and bowed. "I do, King Rhys."

"My reports stated they killed you along with your father when Lord Cameron claimed the throne of Sacia."

"Your reports were almost correct. I was very close to death."

"You look well for someone on the brink of death."

"That is a complicated story, your Majesty. I barely escaped the palace the night my father died, but a stranger helped heal us."

King Rhys raised an eyebrow. "Is that so?" He turned and looked at the other two. "Who are they?"

Liam pointed to each one. "This is Evan, my bodyguard, and Theron, a friend of ours. Sacian guards left Theron for dead after they discovered him seeking information on Cameron."

The king paced back and forth, appearing deep in thought. The three prisoners stood there in silence. Finally, he turned back to Liam. "How did you escape if you were badly injured?"

"The castle has tunnels. Tunnels not even my uncle knew of. He knows of them by now, I'm sure, or some of them at least."

"I see. How do I know you are who you say you are and not some spy or assassin sent by Cameron?"

"I'm afraid I don't have any proof to offer. I would swear on my father's grave that I would not lie to you, your Majesty. My suspicion is Cameron's planning to attack Paelea and with my escape, he may push to attack sooner."

"You don't think he believes you're dead?"

"My uncle is very meticulous. He won't believe I am dead unless he sees my body."

King Rhys turned and looked at his commander. "Did they have weapons when you captured them?"

"They did, sire. As soon as we approached, they laid them down and surrendered."

"I would like to speak more with you, Liam, but that can wait until later. Please forgive me for leaving the chains on you for now. With relations between the two nations once again deteriorated, I cannot take a chance. However, I wish to see you fed. You all look as though you've been through hell. Commander, see them to the dining hall." Rhys then turned back to them.

"After, we shall speak again. I would like to know more. I do want to believe you are the prince."

"I understand, your Majesty. Once again, these are troubled times we live in."

"Indeed."

Chapter Thirty-Two

Raven and Elysia set up camp for the evening, well north of the Sacian castle where the woodlands broke up into patches spread out along a grassy plain. A mountain range to the north had slowly become visible. Raven pointed toward the range.

"Is that where we're going?"

"I'm not sure yet. I have not heard mother's voice in a while."

"Maybe we're already where she wants us and set a trap."

Elysia laughed. "I never imagined you being the paranoid type."

"I'm not, when I know where I'm headed. This waiting around for directions from an invisible entity is a little nerve wrecking."

"She's not an invisible entity, silly. She's our mother, and she's calling us for help."

"No. She's calling you for help. I'm not even sure why I'm following you. The more I think about this, the more insane it sounds."

Elysia responded, but then they both heard rustling to their left. Raven held up a finger to her mouth and listened. Suddenly they heard it from all sides and whatever they were, surrounded them. Raven unsheathed her sword, ready for whatever was coming toward them. Elysia's eyes turned purple, and she raised her hands, violet energy wrapping around her. Raven saw it first. Eyes peering from the darkness. Elysia saw two more sets of eyes to her right. Raven spit.

"Are these what I think they are?"

"Their eyes look like those of demon wolves."

"Aren't they just myths?"

Elysia gave her a quick look. "Do they look like myths to you?"

"I guess not."

Elysia rolled her magic in her hands and then stretched it out into a whip. She swung it side to side, daring the wolves to approach any closer.

"Can I do that?" Raven asked.

"I'm not sure. Your magic differs from mine. If you can control your anger, now would be a good time to test it."

Raven sheathed her sword. She looked nervously at her hands, remembering she almost killed herself the last time her magic appeared. Closing her eyes, she concentrated and allowed her anger to surface. She felt her arms heat up and when she opened her eyes, she saw the flames wrapping around her wrists. They could hear the wolves growling, as more reddish eyes appeared all around them.

"We're definitely surrounded." Raven stating the obvious.

"Are you ready, sister?"

"Ready, Elysia." She still hadn't bought into the sister part yet and definitely not the mother part either, but knew she needed her help to get them out of this.

Elysia cracked her whip toward the darkness and could hear the footsteps stop for a moment, as if they were sizing up their prey. Raven knew she needed to be careful, or she would set the whole patch of woods on fire. She concentrated on keeping her magic under control. Raven sensed several wolves on her left and they attacked. She faced them as they came at her while she concentrated and shot firebolts at them. Both hit their targets, and she could hear them yelp and whimper as they ran back into the darkness. A third one sprang at her and pushed her to the ground, teeth gnashing at her. Drool fell from its mouth and burned her skin where it landed. She pushed the beast off and released another firebolt, hitting it square in the chest and knocking it to the ground.

Raven glanced over at Elysia, who was warding off several with her magic. She was using the whip in one hand and what appeared to be purple lightning from her other hand. She wasn't even breaking a sweat where Raven was struggling to keep her magic contained. As more wolves came toward her, her anger intensified, causing her magic to follow suit. This time, two wolves charged and were fully engulfed in flames. Elysia shot a look over at her and yelled for her to calm down. Raven tried, but her anger seemed to take over. Before she knew it, a dozen of the demon wolves lay dead around her. She felt her arms burning and Raven screamed as the pain she had felt before returned. Elysia disposed of the last wolf attacking her and then concentrated her magic to surround Raven. A purple aura pulsated around Raven, and she relaxed, her fire magic subsiding. When Elysia decided she had calmed down enough, she released her magic and turned to see no more of the wolves around them. The ones that weren't dead retreated to where they had come from. Raven collapsed to the ground and looked at her arms. They were singed but nothing like before.

"You're getting better." Elysia noted.

"Yeah, but I needed you to calm me down before I went completely out of control."

"True, but you could control it for a little while. You just need to learn patience to control your anger. That is where you are losing it."

"I'm trying. I guess I have more built up in me than I reali— Elysia?"

Elysia suddenly stared straight ahead, and her eyes glossed over.

"Mother has contacted me again. She's impressed with our abilities and how far along you have come."

"That's nice. What does she want?"

"We are to travel to the mountains toward the north. There will be a trail that winds up the mountainside. Once we're on the trail, she will guide us further."

"Why not just tell us where we need to go? Why all the secrecy? Can she hear me?"

"She can hear you, Raven. She says you are just as stubborn as you used to be. So headstrong."

"Well, you can tell her if that's really mother, she made me this way by LEAVING!"

"Raven, please don't talk to our mother like that. She needs our help."

Raven watched Elysia. Her eyes were still glossed over. "Is that you speaking, or her?"

"Both actually. We need to trust her."

"You should know me by now, *sister*. I'm more of a verify, then trust kind of gal."

"You will learn, Raven. She can be trusted, just as you trust me."

"Just because you've helped me doesn't mean I trust you. I still know nothing about you."

Her eyes returned to normal, and she looked at Raven. "You still don't trust me, yet you are following me to a destination you don't even know."

"Honestly, I can't believe I'm doing this myself. It's more so I can learn to control my magic than to see someone or something claiming to be our mother.”

“She’s not claiming to be. I can feel the connection now. She’s real, Raven. She is our mother!”

“Stop it! Just stop! You’ve never even met her. You were just a baby, and she left or died or whatever. I’m betting you don’t even know what she looks like, yet you say you have a connection.”

“Through magic, Raven. That’s how.”

“Then why isn’t she connecting with me? I have known her the longest, if she is who she says she is.”

“Because your magic is new to you. You barely have any control. Once you are tuned to it, you will understand.”

“Whatever. So, we’re headed north. Let’s go then and put this to rest once and for all.”

Elysia shook her head. “No.”

“Excuse me?”

“If you are going to have that attitude toward our mother, then you can’t come with me. She needs our help, but you have to promise me one thing.”

“And that is?”

“You must keep an open mind, Raven. If you refuse to believe she is who she says she is, I will give you all the knowledge I can right now to help you control your magic. If you can’t have an open mind, you must not come any further.”

Raven stared at Elysia. She noticed the woman was changing right in front of her. She was less a person who was cheerful and quirky, to more of someone who dealt with absolutes. Elysia appeared possessed, as if the person she was connecting with was slowly controlling her. She had to see this through, if nothing else, to make sure Elysia did nothing that would harm herself. Raven took a deep breath and sighed.

“I promise I will try to do better to keep an open mind. I realize how important this is to you.”

Elysia looked as if trying to read her mind. “Fine, you can come. I want you there, Raven, when we awaken her. It will be beautiful.”

“I can’t wait to see this.” Raven wasn’t even lying. She knew what they were heading into might be dangerous, but she would be ready. She would continue to hone her magic. If nothing else, it would give her an extra weapon to use. She could also change her personality as well. She learned that skill to get closer to her targets.

Now she would use it to throw off Elysia.

"Thank you, Elysia."

"For what?"

"For bringing me along. I have already learned so much from you. I promise to be more understanding in the future."

Elysia smiled at her. Not the smile Raven was used to, though. It was… different. She wasn't sure why, but she filed it into her memory with the rest of the changes she was seeing. Elysia said not another word. She gathered her things together and began walking north. Raven followed her in silence.

Chapter Thirty-Three

King Cameron stood on the south castle wall overlooking the meadow. The size of the army gathering impressed him. Cameron knew a good portion was green and had never seen combat, but they would suffice as sacrificial lambs. He hadn't told them for obvious reasons. His speech to his army was about strength in numbers and that each one of them were protectors of Sacia, and that to protect their homeland, they must take the fight to the Paeleans. With their sheer numbers, they would be victorious over the battle-weary elves.

He turned to his closest aide, Luther. "Far too long, we've had to battle a nemesis that has destroyed our homes and our farmland. I intend to crush them no matter where the battle is, and it will only be the beginning."

"The beginning, milord?" Luther asked.

"Yes, I intend to reunite the ancestral lands of Sacia to form a united kingdom. This way, we can thwart any threat that might loom beyond our borders. We will be respected and feared."

"That's a bold vision you have, your Majesty."

"You do not agree?"

"On the contrary, I believe it is genius. Many of us have dreamed of a strong Sacia where peace reigned. If our foes fear us, they will not attack. You will be one of the greatest kings Sacia has ever seen."

Cameron loved the sound of that. He would do what he felt was necessary to ensure Sacia's future. He watched over the army below and smiled. Yes, he would be the *greatest* Sacian king ever. Even Liam or Raven could not stop him now. The battle for Sacia's homeland would begin tomorrow.

Chapter Thirty-Four

Guards escorted Liam to King Rhys's chamber while they kept Evan and Theron in the dining hall. Evan protested, but Rhys assured him no harm would come to any of them, so long as they cooperated.

"Prove to me, Liam, that you are who you say you are. I want to believe you."

"I'm afraid all I can offer is my word. My father was King Warrick. He had grown suspicious of my uncle and was watching him closely after the bounty hunter had escaped with her prisoner."

"Do you believe this man murdered your emissary?"

"I do not, your highness. I believe Cameron set him up to undo the peace treaty my father had forged with you."

Rhys leaned back in his chair, watching Liam's movements. Either he was so trained as to not betray himself, or he was who he said he was.

"Why come here? To me? Surely you must have thought I would think you were a spy."

"I had to take that chance. I know Cameron will start yet another war with the Paeleans and that is not what I want to see happen. I am the rightful heir of Sacia, but he knew I would continue what my father started, and that is why he tried to have me killed."

"So, you would fight with us against your own people?"

"Yes. Unfortunately, my uncle has everyone convinced that Sacia will not be safe until Paelea is destroyed. Not just defeated, but eliminated."

King Rhys raised an eyebrow at that statement. "Are you certain of this? My informants have told me he wants to restart the war, but you say he wishes for us to be wiped out completely?"

"I'm afraid so, your Majesty. Ever since my mother died, Cameron has blamed Paelea, and his hatred has driven him mad."

"This is troublesome. This war has already decimated both sides, yet he wishes to continue this and to attack us directly here." Rhys looked hard at Liam. "I believe you, Liam. I can see the pain in your eyes. Tell me, how would you wish us to use you?"

"On the front lines. If enough soldiers see me that is not brainwashed by Cameron, they might waver and even join with us."

Liam grew silent for a moment.

"May I ask you a question, your Majesty?"

"Yes. What do you wish to know?"

"If Paelea defeats Cameron, what fate awaits Sacia?"

"Excellent question. You wish to replace Cameron as leader of Sacia."

"I do, and I would gladly accept any safeguards to prevent another war between our kingdoms, at least in our lifetimes. Perhaps by then, a lasting peace would be instilled for the next generation."

"You are wise beyond your years, Prince Liam. I think we could negotiate a settlement should we succeed. I didn't know your father, but I sensed him to be a good man."

Liam looked away for a moment. Tears welled up in his eyes, but he refused to surrender to them. "He was a good man, and in the small time he was king, he respected you."

"What about the situation with my scout, Erinoth? He was brought to Sacia under suspicion of murder. Erinoth would never murder anyone. He was simply a scout and would only kill in self-defense."

"My father wished only to speak with him, to learn the truth. The bounty hunter had orders to bring Erinoth directly to him, as he knew very well what Cameron might do. I am certain my uncle had him framed, just from speaking with Raven."

"The bounty hunter," Rhys added.

"Yes, she told me this herself."

"I met her when both she and Erinoth arrived. I pray she is doing well."

"I heard she foolishly went after Cameron while we were still healing up, but we have heard nothing else. Since Cameron seems to be still alive, I fear he may have killed her as well."

"She's resourceful. I wouldn't believe it until you learn otherwise."

Rhys stood up, and Liam rose with him and bowed.

"I will consider your request and discuss it with Commander Paro. Rest tonight. We began our journey to Sacia in the morning. We will not allow them to attack here. Should they reach this far, we will all be dead.”

“I agree they must not reach this far. Thank you for allowing me to speak with you, your Majesty. We will await your decision.”

Liam bowed and then headed back to his friends. Rhys called over Aeson. “Gather the commanders for a short meeting. I want them to know about Liam’s inclusion in our plans. He might actually become a firm ally once this struggle has concluded.”

“Yes, milord.” Aeson bowed and closed the door behind him.

Chapter Thirty-Five

"Mother, we're getting closer." Elysia focused on the path before them and all but ignoring Raven now. Raven would occasionally ask her generalized questions and Elysia would answer as needed, but she no longer looked directly at her sister.

Raven regretted coming with Elysia. In the beginning, she thought it would be her and Elysia against whoever was claiming to be their mother. 'Their' mother.

Where did that come from? Raven pondered. Did she believe she had a sister now? She had already opened herself up to the possibility, but now she was subconsciously thinking it to be so.

They wound up the mountainside. The weather deteriorated as they climbed. At the base, it was sunny, but they could see the clouds rolling in. What began as steady rain now turned into heavy snow. The wind was light, and Raven hoped it stayed that way, but she wasn't holding her breath. The higher up they went, the worse the storm became.

"You shouldn't be so negative, Raven. Why can't you accept that this is our mother?"

Raven glanced at Elysia. She still did not look at her. However, she seemed to speak to her now instead of at her.

"I was forced to survive. Doing so meant not trusting people. I could have easily gone the path of an outlaw, or worse. Instead, I hunted them down. Doing so gave me the freedom to release anger, but lawfully. It might not have been the ideal life for a woman, but it kept me sane. As for this idea that 'our' mother is up here, I already told you I am keeping an open mind. You must forgive me, though, if I find it hard to believe. I'm still trying to figure you out as well. You must admit, I've come a long way over the last couple of weeks."

"I admit you have opened up since our first encounter." Elysia turned and looked at Raven, or rather she seemed to look through her and gave her another empty smile. "You will see this is our mother. We will save her from the hold this dragon has on her, and we can be a family again."

"And this darkness you mentioned was coming?"

Elysia seemed to shake herself from her trance, and this time, looked Raven right in the eyes. "The darkness IS the dragon. Our mother is the vessel to stop the dragon."

Raven nodded at Elysia and said no more. She would just have to be ready should the situation deteriorate. Elysia could not be persuaded that this woman who claimed to be their mother might be a liar.

Chapter Thirty-Six

At first light, the Sacian army was readying for battle. As the garrisons all aligned in formation, the king rode to the middle to address everyone.

"The day has come when Sacia reclaims our ancient lands, foolishly given away through mistakes in the past! We will return to glory and show the rest of the realm that we will be feared and respected! We will succeed because the greatest warriors have trained you! Trust your brothers-in-arms as they will have your back! Do not fear death! Death in battle is most glorious, and songs will be written about your courage! We will end this war once and for all so that we may see real peace! Once the battle begins, we will take no hostages! Kill everyone except King Rhys! He will be the last Paelean to be executed! An enemy left alive is an enemy that will seek revenge in the future! Onward to Paelea! God be with us in our righteous endeavor!"

The men erupted in cheers, and the king raised his sword and marched forward. The army commanders followed suit and the army of Sacia began their march toward Paelea. Stretched out across the meadow ten thousand strong, everyone marched in unity, confident and eager to fight and to die for their new king. The front line comprised foot soldiers armed with spears, swords, and shields. Several hundred archers followed the foot soldiers. Five hundred well-armed cavalry followed behind them. Siege equipment followed with the remaining army and light calvary amassed behind everyone. These included the more seasoned soldiers, along with newer recruits that showed great promise. From atop his horse, King Cameron smiled as his army inched toward their destination.

*****

"Forgive me, my king. Are you sure we can trust Liam?" Commander Paro Gestured toward the Sacian prince. "He is Sacian, and we are about to go to war yet again with his people."

"I understand your concerns, commander. I had the same concerns myself, but Liam and his friends came to us battered from escaping their homeland. He has given us valuable information, and I would not be surprised if the Sacian army were on their way as we speak. He has valid reasons for siding with us as Cameron murdered his father. Perhaps, if his own people see he is still alive, they will realize they have been deceived. If not, he will die for us so that Cameron will not continue his reign."

Liam stepped forward. "Your Majesty, may I say something?"

King Rhys nodded. "Speak freely."

"I know my friends and I come to you as strangers. We are from the enemy, which comes to destroy you. My uncle betrayed and murdered my father. Cameron has convinced my people that I am dead. He even sent out assassins to prevent us from coming here. I know the common people of Sacia are as tired of war as you are. Cameron possesses the gift of speech and has likely convinced them that your defeat is necessary for peace. I regret I must fight against my brethren, but hopefully I can convince them to turn on Cameron before any more blood flows. If I cannot do so, I will fight to preserve Paelea, as you deserve the right to be free. You should no longer be fearful that your neighbors will be in constant war with you. Therefore, if this fight is necessary, Evan, Theron, and I would be honored to fight alongside noble people like yourself. Once this is over and Paelea is victorious, I will then make my pledge to King Rhys to rebuild Sacia as firm allies to Paelea if he so allows."

Commander Paro nodded at Liam. "I hear the honesty in your voice. I don't believe you will be successful in preventing this war that King Cameron thirsts for, but you are all welcome to fight beside me. One word of warning, Prince Liam. Should you dare try to betray us, justice will be swift."

Liam bowed his head. "I understand, commander."

Paro turned to Rhys. "With that settled, we are ready, my king."

"Very good, commander." Rhys, already mounted on his stallion, moved to the front of his army.

"It saddens me that once more we must head into battle. This time, however, we are not just trying to defeat an enemy, we are fighting for our own survival. Sacia means to extinguish us from our lands. If we must fight to our last man, then so be it! Paelea will live on! We shall be victorious! I want to say before we begin, I am already proud of each and every one of you. If you can fight once more beside me, we cannot be defeated. May God bless our cause!"

The soldiers raised their fists and erupted in raucous applause. Commander Paro took over and shouted his orders. The Paelean warriors all took their positions and, with a nod from King Rhys, Paro raised his sword and pointed forward. The army began their march toward Sacia. If they win, they will return to their homeland victorious. Lose, however, and Paelea would be no more.

Chapter Thirty-Seven

The wind howled, and the air became colder and thinner as they climbed. The path was treacherous, but the two women had few issues other than slipping a couple of times. They had prepared well enough for the journey, so they pushed on, stopping a few times to rest either in shallow caves or overhangs to protect them from the wind. Elysia wanted to push on, but Raven convinced her they needed rest and that hopefully the storm would ease up a bit. Her sister relented but complained constantly about finishing their journey. Whatever hold the woman had on Elysia was getting stronger the closer they got to the summit. Raven knew if this person was an imposter, she may have to fight both women. She wasn't sure how she would break the mind control Elysia was under, but Raven would figure something out.

"Just up ahead and around the corner will be the last stretch," Elysia noted. "There is a building carved into the mountain. Mother is there."

"That is good to hear. I'm ready to get out of this weather. The snow is really piling up now."

"The tougher the journey, the stronger it makes you as a person." Elysia smiled, but still not the smile Raven knew. It was that empty smile, almost like it wasn't even hers at all.

As they continued, the sisters trudged around the corner, practically digging their way through snowdrifts. The wind was ferocious now, and Raven feared it could whisk them off the mountain at any moment. Once they got through the snowdrifts and around another corner, the wind eased up considerably. She could hear it howling behind her still, but it was only a breeze now. While thankful for it, this just caused Raven's senses to stir. Up ahead, the path widened, and the summit was more like a plateau than a peak. In the middle, rock spires jutted upward, and she could see the building Elysia had mentioned. What was a cave entrance at one time was now stone blocks with a weathered wooden door. Elysia wasted no time investigating and walked right up to the door. Raven followed hesitantly behind her, watching for traps.

"We're here!" Elysia shouted with pure joy.

"We should investigate before just barging in." Raven advised.

"Nonsense! If there were anything to be wary of, mother would have mentioned it to me."

"That's true, I guess." Raven shook her head. "Well, let's go in."

Elysia grabbed the handle and pulled on the door. Surprising to Raven, there was no lock, and the door opened easily, despite the harsh conditions this high up.

Elysia walked in and glanced behind her. "Coming sister?"

Raven steadied herself and nodded. As she walked through the door, she noticed the torches on the wall lit. She grabbed Elysia's arm.

"If mother's in trouble, there is probably a trap set for us. We must be careful."

"There's no need to be fearful now, sister. Mother is just upstairs. She lit these torches to show us the way."

"She's walking around?"

"No silly! She used her magic. She cannot come to us. We must go to her and free her from her bonds."

Raven was really concerned now. She was new to magic, but she was certain someone who could use mind control and light torches while bound could be extremely dangerous. She had better control of her power now but could not match up with a powerful sorceress. Her gut was telling her to run, but her stubbornness would not let her. She had to see this person for herself and somehow break the hold she had on Elysia. She also had to know if there was really some sort of evil headed for their realm. Then she would figure out an escape plan. For now, against her better judgment, she followed her sister up to the top of the stairs. A long hallway stretched to the left, and Elysia pointed to the door at the end. "Mother is there! We made it Raven! You will see the journey was worth it."

"I pray you're right, Elysia. The alternative may be deadly."

Elysia laughed. "Always the pessimist. We'll have to change your attitude."

"This attitude has kept me alive all these years."

"That and your untapped magic."

"So it may seem."

Raven and Elysia walked to the end of the hallway. As they both looked at each other, Raven knew their lives would never be the same. Elysia reached for the handle and opened the door.

Chapter Thirty-Eight

Irsei circled the town she had just incinerated. Her mind was confused. She didn't understand why she burned the whole town and the people in it. Most escaped, but some didn't. Sorrow and guilt took over, and she flew off to a nearby peak and slowly remembered everything.

A little over five hundred years ago, Irsei exacted vengeance against this part of the realm, killing those who hunted her. She took the fight to the castles of each kingdom and even surrounding villages. The kingdom of Garus, hearing of the dragon attacks from refugees of a nearby kingdom, set a trap for her and Irsei was nearly killed. She was severely injured but escaped and fled to the far north regions. Irsei went as far as she could go before finally losing consciousness. She awoke on a ledge high atop the Silverfrost range. She was shocked to still be alive and spent months recovering from her injuries. The dragon then decided she no longer had a thirst for vengeance. Abundant food and water sustained her in this remote region, far away from any human settlement. She found she enjoyed the solace of her isolation… until SHE came. Her thoughts drifted back a couple of months to recall when her life was no longer her own.

SHE was a powerful sorceress and must have tracked her during her trips to hunt for food. Irsei woke up one morning, unable to move. All she could do was stare at a human with an evil grin on her face.

"I guess you are wondering how and why you are in this… compromising position."

The woman ran her right hand along the side of Irsei's scaly green and gold skin.

"I heard all the rumors about a green and gold dragon that once reigned terror upon the realm. The townspeople were scared and knew they had to stop these devastating attacks. A massive trap was set for the dragon, and it was killed. Everyone lived happily ever after, or so the story goes."

The woman tapped her chin as if in deep thought.

"The problem I kept having with this tale is that they never found a dragon. Now one would think either the entire story was a fairy tale, or the dragon was still alive. I mean, if they had killed a legendary dragon, especially one so bloodthirsty as mentioned in the stories, one would imagine the bones would be on display in all the kingdoms, and the head would be a decoration piece in a king's throne room."

The woman walked back to where Irsei could see her again. "My guess was if this dragon was indeed real and had escaped, it might go somewhere it wouldn't be found or even searched for. I must admit, it was quite the journey to find you. I applaud your efforts to conceal yourself. After five hundred years, one would understand letting their guard down for unwanted guests."

The woman paused for a moment to admire the prize in front of her.

"Now comes the 'why' I've come for you. I need that ferociousness of yours to come out and play once more. I need retribution and you would be an excellent weapon for that."

Irsei tried to break whatever grip this woman had on her, but she couldn't move at all.

"There's no point in trying to move. I assure you this spell is quite powerful and even a grand dragon won't be able to break its hold. My next spell will allow me to control you when that need arises. So, enjoy your peace and isolation for now. When I need you, I will call, and you will do my bidding. I will also be in your mind, so we will converse once the spell has taken hold. Once it does, the spell keeping you in place will end and you can move around once again. Goodbye dragon. You will hear from me soon."

Irsei snapped herself back to the present and sighed. She watched the town in flames off in the distance and grew angry at the witch who forced her to do this. She didn't know how she would break this spell, but she would try.

The witch reached out to her; her will was no longer her own. She knew what she was doing, but she could not stop herself. Dragons, mostly, were immune to magic, but this woman was more powerful than any witch she had ever known. Guilt ran through her, and she could no longer watch what was left of the town. Sadly, Irsei spread her wings and flew back to her ledge in the Silverfrost mountains to rest. She watched the clouds race by. A storm was coming, but that did not bother the dragon. Her skin could withstand the coldest and harshest of storms. Her mind, however, could not shake the grip of the witch. A few hours passed, and she saw the ledge where she called home. She wondered if she could fly far enough away to break this spell. Irsei soared past the ledge and continued farther north. She flew until she thought she was far enough away, but she again heard the voice.

Running away from me, dragon? We still have unfinished business, my pet.

"I am not your pet! Leave me in peace! I've done your bidding!"

Peace? There will be no peace until I have had my revenge. The town you burned; I went to them for mercy. They showed me none. Therefore, they received no mercy in return. Sacia and Paelea are next. Those fools only know war and while they are distracted trying to kill each other, you will destroy them both. But first, I have a more immediate situation that needs tending to. Fly as far away as you wish, my pet. You will never be too far that I can't rein you in. You can be sure that I will call on you when I need you and you will have no choice but to obey.

Irsei found an isolated valley and landed. Tired and angry, she thought about finding a cliff nearby and just walking off the edge and ending her life. Then the witch could no longer use her as a weapon. Irsei knew, however, the sorceress would never allow her to do so. She might be punished for attempting to kill herself. No, Irsei knew there was no escape. Not until the sorceress was finished with her. *If* she finished with her. Instead, the dragon just laid down in the soft grass of the valley and watched various fish jump in a nearby stream. She listened to the sounds all around her and sighed. After a while, she flew back to her ledge on the side of the mountain. She laid down, closed her eyes, and slept. She dreamed of the time she was young and unaware of what her future held. A tear streamed down her face and trickled to the ground.

Chapter Thirty-Nine

Elysia and Raven stood before the stone table and stared at the sight before them. A woman laid on the table dressed in a red gown with her hands folded on her stomach. Around her was some sort of barrier that glowed a golden color yet was transparent. The woman appeared to be dead but was obviously in a deep sleep. She looked over at Elysia, who had tears streaming down her cheeks.

"Do you see her, Raven? Do you not recognize our mother?"

Raven stepped forward to get a better look. Looking at the woman up close, she suddenly froze. Memories of her mother rushed to her all at once. She remembered the house they lived in, all the things she was taught and the day she was forced to leave when her mother did not return from town one day. The sudden recollection of that memory caused Raven to lose her balance, but Elysia caught her. Raven turned to Elysia and looked back at… her mother. She could see the resemblance between the two. Elysia was right all along. They were… are sisters. A thousand questions ran through her head now. Like: *Why did she leave all of those years ago?* And: *Why she was here now?* There were the only two questions she cared about at the moment.

Raven pulled away from Elysia's grip. She looked around and found an old torch lying on the ground.

"What are you doing, Raven?" Elysia asked curiously.

"I need to see something." Raven picked up the torch and touched the barrier between them and their mother. Sparks sizzled, and the wood smoked. "That's what I thought. It's impenetrable. I don't suppose she told you how to break the spell."

Elysia shook her head. "Since we arrived, she hasn't spoken another word to me."

Raven felt her skin tingle and spun around. Unsheathing her sword, she saw two demon wolves' approach. Behind them, several more entered the room, growling at them. As Raven stepped forward to attack, she heard a familiar voice behind her.

"Don't Raven. They will only attack if I tell them to."

Raven and Elysia both spun around to see their mother sitting up and the barrier reshaping itself as if allowing her to move.

"Mother? You are controlling them?" Raven asked.

"I am, daughter." She laughed. "It is good to see you again."

Raven glanced over at her sister and realized Elysia was not going to attack the wolves. She was facing Raven. Elysia had her magic wrapped around her hands, ready to strike. Raven glared at her sister and then turned back to her mother.

"Is it? By the look of my sister and these wolves, I find it hard to believe."

"It's… complicated. I am delighted to see you, but I can feel your distrust in all of this. People I once cared for threatened and betrayed me. Forgive me if I'm more prepared this time."

"Well, you must forgive my distrust, mother. You left me and I was told you were dead. I was only a child, and I grieved for a long time for you. I was left to make my own way, and I learned to survive. No thanks to you."

"Raven!" Elysia cut in. "Do not talk to our mother this way."

Raven pointed at Elysia. "It's one thing to control a wolf's mind, but what you are doing to Elysia is why I'm having a hard time with this. Explain yourself to me and release Elysia. Why do you need to use her? Are you in such a weakened state that I'm a threat to you?"

"You're right, dear, I don't need her."

Elysia looked down at her hands. She immediately pulled her magic back in and shook her head. "What happened?"

Raven fixed her eyes on her mother while she spoke to Elysia. "You just weren't yourself is all. Are you okay?"

"Yeah, I think so."

"So, spill it, Lisabet! Why are you imprisoned here? Or are you in trouble at all?"

Lisabet sighed when Raven called her by her name instead of mother. She paused for a moment and explained.

"Years ago, when you were a child, magic was condemned in this realm as it still is today. The previous war saw many people die at the hands of those with gifts. A decree was soon declared, and anyone caught performing any type of magic not sanctioned by the court would be punished. By punished, they meant persecuted. Something caught me healing a boy who had fallen over a shallow cliff face. He had a nasty head wound and would have died were it not for me. That person saw what I was doing and reported me. They ignored that I had saved the boy and focused instead on how I did it."

"They imprisoned you for aiding a boy? There must be more to the story than this," Raven responded skeptically.

"No, my child. We were forbidden to use our magic under any circumstances. In fact, the kingdoms in this realm wanted to kill anyone with magic outside of their control. I tried to escape before they captured me. I made my way up to Hitus, hoping for sanctuary with the dwarves. They hid me for a while until pressure was brought upon them to hand me over to Sacia. The king hid me in a merchant's caravan and told Sacia I had escaped. I left the caravan in Garus. The kingdom was beyond here, in the northern part of this realm, and I begged them for mercy, vowing to never use magic again. They accepted me into their kingdom, or so I thought."

"For months, I worried Sacia would discover my location and demand they hand me over, but they never did. I was blending in and making a new life for myself. I befriended a man in town and thought that I would live the rest of my life in peace. He asked for my hand in marriage, and I accepted. After the wedding, I moved to his place outside of town. It was a beautiful home, made of stone from the nearby mountains. He had so much land that I felt completely isolated from the outside world. I had found my peace for which I had been searching. One night, however, several men snuck into our home while we were sleeping and killed my husband. By the time I realized what had happened, another sorcerer spelled me, rendering me unconscious. When I awoke, I tried to break free, but the sorcerer had neutralized my magic. We were on the way back to Sacia for me to face judgment. The man left to meet with the king, but not before leaving me in this shell. He was much more powerful than I, and he placed a hibernation spell on me so that I could not escape. I have just recently awakened, and it is obvious seeing you two that I have been asleep for many years. I'm unsure of why he never returned, but my body is weak, and I need nourishment soon, before I rapidly deteriorate."

Raven soaked in her story and raised an eyebrow. "You say you have been here for years asleep, with no food or water, and yet you are still alive?"

Elysia chimed in. "I've heard of hibernation spells. They slow your body to where you can survive several years with no food or water. It will also slow the aging process, which is why she has hardly aged at all throughout the years. However, once the spell is weakened or lifted, your body returns to normal, and one must find nourishment within a certain amount of time, or the body will start declining in health."

"You are correct, my child. I can already feel I am growing weak."

Raven pointed behind her. "Yet you are strong enough to call these animals to protect you."

"You do not believe me."

"I believe you are trapped here. How you are controlling these animals and summoning Elysia in such a weakened state is a valid concern."

"I don't know either, but I am. Most of my strength was used to summon Elysia. I used the last of it to summon the wolves. I had to make sure it was you two and not some intruders. I see you two are getting along, okay."

Raven looked over at Elysia, who was beaming at her, and rolled her eyes. "Yeah, that's still a work in progress." Raven returned her attention to Lisabet. "Why did you not summon me?"

"I could sense her magic, but not yours. I am glad you came along, though. It is good to see my daughters again."

Raven ignored that last part. "So, what now? I know I can't break this spell, and I doubt Elysia can, either."

"Actually, I think I can," Elysia chimed in. "Especially with you here Raven, I can draw upon your magic to break this spell."

Raven grabbed her sister by the arm and pulled her away. "Are you sure about this? I know she is our mother, but we know nothing of this woman. She could be lying to us."

"She would not lie to us. We are her daughters. Besides, between the two of us, we could control her in her weakened state."

"You know my intuition is screaming at me right now. I'm never wrong about these things."

Elysia smiled at her sister. "Well, I think you are this time. We'll be fine."

Raven let go of Elysia and looked back at her mother. Lisabet smiled at her.

"Are you satisfied, daughter?"

"Not even close, but for her sake, I will help."

"Thank you, Raven."

Raven turned back to Elysia. "What do you need?"

"Just stand here to my left and grab my hand. With your blessing, I am going to tap into your magic and combine it with mine. Together, we should be able to overwhelm the spell."

"That sounds easy enough. Go ahead then."

Elysia held out her hand, and Raven reluctantly grabbed it. "Just remember, I said this is a mistake."

Elysia chuckled. "You're just being paranoid, as usual."

Elysia closed her eyes and chanted. Raven felt Elysia's magic coursing through her, taking over. She watched her right arm rise to match her sister's left arm. Raven kept her eyes open to watch her mother's every move. She just sat at the table with her legs crossed and her head tilted back, eyes closed. Elysia continued chanting, and Raven watched as Elysia's purple hue mixed with her red, as their magic combined to wrap around the energy field trapping their mother in place.

Raven trembled. She still wasn't used to her magic. It drained her energy, and she felt weak. Elysia tightened her grip and Raven felt renewed strength flowing through her. It was obvious how powerful her sister was, and yet she was easily controlled by their mother. Who were they unleashing onto this world? She decided to stop her sister from finishing the spell, but found she could not move, nor could she speak. She looked at her mother, who was watching her. Could she now read her thoughts? Her mother simply smiled at her and nodded. Raven tried harder but was helpless to do anything. All she could do was wait and hope she was wrong. The way her mother looked at her, though, was worrisome. Her smile was sinister looking. Her mother then closed her eyes and again leaned her head back. Raven could feel Elysia's magic receding and felt herself regaining control of her own body again. As soon as she could, she released her hand from Elysia and stepped back.

The energy surrounding her mother was gone, and Lisabet sat on the edge of the table with her legs dangling off the side. She stretched her arms above her head and smiled. "Thank you, my daughters. I don't know if I can ever repay you for setting me free."

Elysia walked up and hugged Lisabet. Raven could tell she was weak from using so much magic at once.

Raven stayed back. "What will you do now that we released you from this hibernation spell?"

"The first thing I need to do is eat. I'm not sure what I am to do beyond that."

"Fine." Raven turned, pulled out a knife hidden in her boot, turned and threw it into one of the demon wolves, killing it. "I hear the meat's tough, but it's edible."

Lisabet met Raven's eyes. "That will do."

"Good. I will get it skinned and cooked. Watch after Elysia and stay out of her head."

⚜ ⚜ ⚜

Chapter Forty

King Rhys led his army across the plains and well into Sacian territory. They were another half a day, at least before they turned west toward the Sacian kingdom. The midday sun was above them, but off to the south a bit. Spring was in full force and the days were getting longer and warmer. He dreamed of a time as a child before the war had become the way of life in this part of the realm. He thought of friends that were no longer here and of his wife, struck down by a sudden illness not long after their daughter was born. His heart was hardened by all the loss of life the previous war had brought to his people. He was determined to give Paelea a chance at peace without constant threats from Sacia. This battle would be the final one and he hoped it didn't mean Paelea was doomed. If Prince Liam was right, King Cameron wanted not just to defeat them, but to eliminate their race over a misguided prejudice.

King Rhys snapped back to reality as a rider approached. Rhys nodded to Commander Paro, who then ordered the army to halt. Rhys watched the rider as he neared the camp and recognized him at once.

"Erinoth, I presume you have news?"

Erinoth slowed as he neared and bowed his head. "Yes, my king. The Sacians are about a day away."

Rhys looked hard at Erinoth. "Was there something else?"

"Yes, your Majesty. I don't know how, but their numbers are massive. A good number of them, however, appear to be only boys."

Rhys thought for a moment and looked over at Paro. "What do you think of this, commander?"

"It appears King Cameron must have recruited or forced the younger ones into service to protect his more seasoned army, and to give the appearance of a massive force."

"I believe you are right, commander. He means to use them as protection and to thin our front line. He is more devious than I thought. To use boys as interference is unimaginable. We cannot change our plans, however, and it appears the battle will come sooner than expected. We will rest over near the woods, so we will be at full strength when they arrive. Good work, as always, Erinoth. Keep an eye out but mind your surroundings. There is no doubt they have their spies on us as well."

*****

King Rhys approached Liam, Evan, and Theron, sitting by the campfire, discussing the day's events. All three stood and bowed as Rhys approached, and he waved his hands at them.

"You do not need to bow to me. We are all warriors here."

Liam shook his head. "I know there are those who don't believe our intent is to help Paelea and go against Sacia. By bowing, not only does it show the respect you deserve, but it shows others we are here to show loyalty to Paelea. Are we happy about going against our own? Of course not. However, I'm tired of this war as my father was, and I know he held no animosity toward Paelea, nor do I."

Rhys nodded in agreement. "You are wise beyond your years, Prince Liam. It saddens me that I never got to meet your father. He was the first to reach out with an olive branch. I don't know why people can hold such hatred in their hearts, but it seems your uncle is against Paelea. I am honored to have you all fighting alongside us."

"I'm still dealing with the idea that my uncle wants me dead. His hatred for Paelea is driving him mad."

"Mad men have long caused wars since the beginning of time. I have always believed men with a good conscience could discuss and find solutions to any problem. Evil men ignore reason and rely strictly on their own feelings and obsessions. We will somehow rise above this and defeat your uncle. Not because of arrogance, but because we must, to survive. Rest now, for tomorrow will decide our fate."

"Yes, your Majesty." Liam bowed and watched as Rhys moved on to another company. As they sat back down, Evan turned to his friend.

"Have you wondered what will happen if we do somehow defeat your uncle?"

Liam stared at the crackling fire in front of him. "What do you mean?"

"If Paelea defeats Sacia, is King Rhys going to just hand the kingdom over to you, or will he claim the lands for Paelea?"

"I don't know. I would not blame the king at all if he absorbed Sacia under Paelea's flag. All the rulers of Sacia outside of my father have always wanted Paelea conquered, and its people enslaved. The fact we are even here among them is proof of Rhys's honor. Whatever happens after this, I will accept. It is time for the bad blood between these two kingdoms to end, and if that means I must lie down my sword and become a common farmer under Paelea, so be it."

Liam looked down at Theron, who was poking at the fire with a stick.

"You've been quiet this whole time. Something on your mind?"

Theron seemed to snap out of a dream. "Oh, sorry. I've just never been in a battle. I've always been behind the walls, safe from any attack."

Evan laid his hand on his shoulder. "You're worried you might not survive."

"Yes, no, I don't know. I almost died before and I wasn't as scared as I thought I would be. I'm more afraid that I will see someone we used to know, and I'll freeze. I'm not sure I can kill someone I know."

Liam nodded at Theron. "That is a valid concern and one I have struggled with as well. The fact is, Cameron has convinced the people of Sacia that this war is a noble cause. The Elven race is nothing more than rats on a ship to him. This part of the realm is the ship, so to speak, and they are coming to exterminate the rats. When the people you call friends see you fighting with the elves, they will hate you and will want your head on a pike. To them, winning this war means killing us all. I can't accept that. You cannot have peace by wiping out an entire race of people. Once you start down that path, your bloodlust will only grow, and you will need more wars to satisfy it. We must stop Cameron and I have grudgingly accepted that people I've known my whole life will stand in the way of that. Rhys's army and we are all that stand in the way of Cameron winning. We cannot allow that to happen! Are you both with me?"

Evan moved and stood beside his friend. "You know I am, Liam. You will make a great king, and I am honored to fight alongside you."

"Well, Evan might just get in the way, so I guess you need me to keep him in line." Theron poked.

"I'm literally standing right here, you know," Evan said.

Liam smirked as he turned to his old friend. "He's not wrong."

"Just keep in mind I will be too busy fighting to save you again."

"Just don't get in the way. I would hate to stab you by accident."

Theron shook his head. "You guys are too much."

*****

The next morning was uneventful as the tents were all packed up and everything else put away. Looking around, you would never have known a battle for their lives would begin today. These seasoned warriors had known war most of their lives, so one more battle didn't seem to faze them one bit.

As the morning faded into afternoon, the three Sacian friends had just finished a late lunch and gathered their things together when the horns sounded. Liam looked solemnly at his friends. "Looks like no sleep tonight. Cameron wants this over with. Let's make him pay for his arrogance."

Liam walked to where King Rhys and Commander Paro were completing their strategy. Paro acknowledged him.

"Are you sure you still want to fight your own people? No one here would think ill of you if you stayed neutral."

"No, commander. This is personal to me. Cameron killed my father and tried to do the same to me and my friends. I'm afraid he might have executed Raven as well. She would have certainly contacted me if she were still alive. We will fight with you until our last breath, if that's what it takes to stop him. Once we are successful and I become the true king of Sacia, I will accept any terms King Rhys proposes, even if it means relinquishing my crown."

Rhys raised an eyebrow at Liam. "You realize what you are saying, yes?"

Liam bowed to Rhys. "I do, your Majesty. Should we win, you will be the victor. Therefore, I will accept your terms, no matter what."

"Very well. Rhys turned his attention to Paro. Shall we ready the men, commander?"

"Yes, my king. They are ready to defend Paelea to the last man."

152

Rhys patted Paro on the back. "Let's pray that will not be necessary, for there will be no more Paelea to defend if that happens."

Chapter Forty-One

Lisabet disappeared into another room and locked the door. She summoned Irsei and told her of her next assignment. *I sense Sacia's army gathering to fight Paelea yet again. Now is the perfect time to engage them. Start at Paelea and don't stop until you reach Sacia. Burn them all! Do not disappoint me, dragon, or I will make you suffer like you have never known.*

Irsei merely nodded, clearly not pleased, but knew she had no choice but to obey. The dragon soared from the cliff and into the clouds, headed toward Paelea.

Smiling, Lisabet exited the room and walked to where Raven was cooking and watched her for a moment before speaking.

"You turned out better than I had hoped, Raven."

"Yeah, no thanks to you."

"That hurts, you know. I never intended to leave you, but the circumstances gave me no choice."

"After you disappeared, my life was pure hell. I had to fight for everything I have. Maybe I should thank you. Had you stuck around, I might have been a weaker version of myself. At least I don't need to depend on anyone. And hey, now I have these powers, so I guess I have you to think about that, I guess. Although I did not know what was happening to me and I almost roasted myself, so again, thanks."

Lisabet sensed Raven's anger building, so she waited a moment before speaking. "I'm sorry. I don't know how many times I have to say it to you before you believe me. You have Elysia now. You can trust her."

"Yeah, I have just recently come to terms that she's my sister, but she's... off, maybe even a little crazy. Plus, it didn't help that you had complete control over her. The closer we came to this place, the worse she got."

Raven stood up and warned her mother. "I better not ever learn that you have done the same to me. I won't be as forgiving as my sister."

"Are you threatening me?"

"Call it what you will. I don't believe someone has trapped you here. I think you're planning something and need Elysia. You weren't betting on me tagging along."

"I don't know what you mean. I am grateful she heard my plea and only entered her mind to guide her here. Believe me, as I would never try to control her directly."

Raven knew she was lying. She stopped pressing the matter and would just watch her closely. She was glad she came now, because she felt she needed to protect Elysia. As much as she thought her sister was not completely sane, she felt she was very naïve toward her mother. Raven would monitor both and then decide what to do next.

"Try to stay out of her mind. Food's done. Let's eat."

❧ ❧ ❧ ❧ ❧

Chapter Forty-Two

Princess Amedee stood at one of the observation points on the wall looking south of Paelea. It was a beautiful, sunny day with a light breeze. She could feel the weather might change at some point, though. No birds were chirping, and she could see clouds building toward the south on the horizon. They rarely went long this time of year without a storm to blow through and try to bring back winter's chill. She closed her eyes and felt the sun warm her face. She would enjoy the pleasant weather while it lasted. After a moment, she turned to head toward the castle. As she started down the steps, she felt a sudden pain in her left arm. She looked down to see where an arrow had grazed her skin and blood trickled down. She ducked as another arrow buzzed overhead. "We're under attack!" She yelled. "Everyone to their stations!" Amedee peered over the wall's edge and saw soldiers spilling from the nearby forest. She heard a voice calling her, and she turned to her right and saw a younger boy heading toward her. She ran over to him. He stopped to grab his breath for a second and pointed to the north. "Siege weapons are coming from the north, milady!"

"The north? How did Sacia move siege equipment that far around so quickly?"

"It's not Sacia. They look like Slestons!"

"Slestons?" Amedee felt dread trying to take over. She shook it away. She needed to focus.

"Gather the bulk of our archers and focus on the siege weapons on the north side! If they get past the wall, we'll be over-matched!"

She noticed a knight coming up to her.

"Speak quickly."

"They are maneuvering a ram to the gate! We need men to focus on holding the doors!"

"Yes! The gates must hold! Any available soldiers and remaining archers, I need some on the wall above the gate! Destroy that ram! The rest of you I need manning the gate! Find anything to support the doors!"

She looked around and saw one of her scouts heading toward the gate.

"Bellas! Come here!"

The scout scurried up the steps to where she was.

"Take a couple of scouts and go through the secret passage and tell my father we are under attack from the Slestons. Make haste and good luck!"

With a quick bow, Bellas hurried back down the stairs and grabbed a couple of scouts and headed off.

"Please be quick," she breathed to herself. She turned to the archers. "I'm headed for the north gate to aid against the siege equipment. You all know what to do. I'll be back as soon as I can."

Amedee ran as fast as she could to her room and grabbed her bow and a quiver of arrows. Anger raged inside her. "We will not give up this castle so easily!" She ran to the stables and grabbed the nearest horse. She didn't even bother with a saddle and hopped on her back and gave a gentle kick. The mare neighed and headed off around the edge of the castle, gaining speed as she raced north. Enemy soldiers hurriedly pushed the siege towers to the walls. Paelean archers let loose a barrage of flame arrows, lighting the towers on fire. Enemy archers returned fire as they placed the trebuchets into positions. Amedee dismounted and scurried up the steps and targeted the ballista operators. One by one she picked them off, her accuracy deadly. She took a moment to watch over the battle. The siege towers were burning, but the Slestons were still trying to climb up and over. Wait. Amedee strained to get a closer look at the soldiers. Those were definitely from the Kingdom of Sleston! Sacia must have made a deal with them. Amedee yelled to those nearest to her.

"More soldiers are coming from the woods!"

Amedee returned her attention to the siege equipment, trying to help keep them at bay. Men were still trying to climb the burning structures, and some were successful while others weren't. Those that made it were killed immediately. The trebuchet's aim was inching closer. Amedee wondered if the walls would hold against the barrage of rocks being hurled at them. The ballistae was another problem altogether. The operators hid behind them and were problematic to hit with their archers.

Amedee ran up to a group of archers. "We need to focus on those ballistae! We need to set them afire!"

"Yes, milady!"

Amedee joined them in raining flaming arrows down on the ballistae and, one by one, they were rendered useless as they burned.

The Slestons put the fires out on the siege equipment. Amedee grew frustrated as she watched the Sleston army grow. As she stopped a moment to collect her thoughts, they threw ladders against the wall. Dozens of ladders with lines of soldiers climbing up and over. She called for every able person to cover the ladders. She pulled her sword and ran to the nearest one. One by one, she either pushed the soldiers off the ladder or killed them with her sword. Others watched as their princess fought with them and they all dug down and fought fiercely beside her, keeping the enemy outside the wall.

Outside the gate, the siege equipment finally stood in ruin, burning to the ground. Seeing no way to penetrate the castle walls, the Sleston army retreated, spreading out, and kept a safe distance from the Paelean archers. They seemed content to keep them trapped within the wall. Perhaps waiting until Sacia appeared and finished the battle. If Sacia did show, that meant her father, King Rhys, was dead and his army destroyed.

Amedee sighed at seeing Sleston withdraw. While she knew they weren't retreating completely, it gave her a chance to check on everyone and see what damage was done. As she descended the steps to return to the south gate, she froze. They had sustained more casualties than she realized. As the dead were carted off and the wounded tended to, she nearly lost her balance at the realization they might not survive this onslaught. Her only hope was the riders, but even she knew they might not deliver the message in time.

Chapter Forty-Three

At Paelea's south wall, the ram continued to weaken the wooden gate. They had set the cover of the ram ablaze several times, but the Sleston soldiers extinguished the flames each time.

Soldiers brought buckets of oil, carefully balancing them so as not to spill. More soldiers near the gate ran and grabbed the buckets, carrying them up the steps. They carried them over to where the ram was and dumped the oil, which splattered all over the cover. A couple of archers lit the top of the ram with flaming arrows, fully engulfing the ram. The heat pouring from the burning ram prevented the Slestons from getting close, and they could only watch in frustration as it burned to the ground.

As the Paeleans cheered, the Sleston soldiers rushed another ram in place. More archers spilled from the forest and rained arrows at the Paelean archers. They ducked for cover, but too many were getting picked off from the sheer volley that was coming at them. In the blink of an eye, the Paeleans knew they were in grave danger.

*****

Amedee continued to survey the area when she heard something off in the distance. She looked around and asked an archer nearby if she had heard the same thing. The archer nodded and stared at the northern sky. The sound grew louder and Amedee rushed back to the top of the wall. She glanced briefly at the Sleston army in the distance, and they too were eying the sky as well. The sound grew louder, almost like a roar.

"It can't be!" Amedee said out loud. She called out to the people below. "Find shelter immediately! Grab anyone hurt and take them with you! Go now!"

Amedee scrambled back down the steps and saw a wounded soldier sitting against the wall, holding his arm. "Can you walk?"

"I-I think so."

"Good! Grab my arm and go as fast as you can!"

"Why? What is that sound?"

Amedee shook her head. "I think it's a dragon!"

Amedee ran to the middle of the north courtyard and grabbed a horn and blew as loud as she could. Everyone turned to look at her with fear in their eyes.

"Everyone to the underground shelter, now!! Grab the wounded as you go! Don't leave anyone who's still alive!"

Amedee looked around and grabbed a soldier running past her and pointed.

"Take my horse and ride as fast as you can to the southern gate and warn the ones there!"

"Yes, milady!"

Amedee watched the horse disappear, turned and saw Portia coming toward her. "You shouldn't be out here! Go to the shelter!"

"Forgive me, milady. I'm not going anywhere without you. You are the one that needs to go. You're our leader while your father is away.

"I will not hide while men, women, and children are still out here!"

"Neither will I then. I will help you get everyone to safety."

Amedee hesitated for a moment, then nodded. As they both ran to help move the wounded, a horn sounded from the center north watchtower. Amedee moved toward the middle of the courtyard and saw a dark object coming closer. Before she could speak, she saw flames and realized it was indeed a dragon! Yes, a dragon! She stood in shock as the creature flew toward her. Standing alone in the center of the courtyard, she found herself frozen in place. She didn't know if it was fear or disbelief, but she just stared at the dragon as it came closer.

"Princess, RUN!" Portia screamed, forcing Amedee out of her trance. She ran the moment the dragon released another spray of fire, and suddenly felt her skin burning. A couple of knights grabbed her, dropping her to the ground. They rolled her in the dirt and grass to put out her burning clothes. The knights then picked up the princess and carried her as fast as they could. As she screamed in pain. Portia hurried behind them until they were safely inside the shelter. The knights laid Amedee down on the ground, and Portia looked over at the damage. She held a secret to everyone but Amedee: she was a sorceress. Amedee helped her keep her secret, as magic was forbidden in the realm. She used her magic more for healing than anything else and hid it in the herbs and other ingredients she made her concoctions with. Now though, her secret was about to come out as she knew the princess was so badly burned, she might not make it. She refused to allow this to happen. She looked up at the knights and pointed across the room.

"In the far cupboard, there are bottles of herbs. Bring them all to me!"

Two of the townspeople near the cupboard heard her request and grabbed all the bottles and set them down by Portia. She grabbed one bottle and poured some in her hand. She then asked for another specific bottle and motioned for the person to pour some of that into her hand as well.

Portia looked at the herbs in her hand and waited for a moment. She was nervous to reveal herself, as she knew what the ramifications would be. Now though, as the princess lay on the ground dying, she had no choice but to act and whatever happened afterward, she would just accept. She closed her eyes and cupped her hands together. She focused her magic and sent it into the herbs. Portia heard gasps in the crowd as her hands glowed a golden color. She didn't even open her eyes to address those around her.

"If you want our princess to live, allow me to do this. I am sworn to her as you are. She is burned too badly to survive normal medicine."

She opened her hands to reveal a paste that she rubbed over Amedee's burned skin. Amedee groaned and writhed in pain, but as the paste covered her skin, she calmed down. For a moment her eyes opened and looked at Portia, but then closed again and her head tilted to one side.

"She killed her!" someone from the crowd exclaimed.

"No, she's resting. These burns will take a while to heal, and you will all see that she will recover."

"A while?" A guard retorted. "It will take months for her burns to heal, if she even survives." He grabbed Portia by the arm and pulled her away from the princess.

"Don't" Amedee faintly whispered. "She stays."

The crowd murmured among themselves. The guard paused a

moment but released Portia and she returned to Amedee's side.

"Help… others," she whispered. She looked at the crowd. "I… command you all… To let her… help."

Chapter Forty-Four

Outside, Irsei roared over the Paelean kingdom. She breathed fire and scorched the land below and watched as people ran for cover. She then flew beyond the walls and spotted her next target, at least the target forced onto her by Lisabet. When she tried to resist, she felt pain spread throughout her body. Giving in, she flew toward what she perceived to be the Sacian army, torching them and the land below her. They tried to run and escape, but beyond the walls of the castle, there was nowhere to go except into the forest. Irsei burned the landscape and the army as well until there was no one left but a few individuals who made it deeper into the forest.

Well done so far, my pet. Continue and finish what I have commanded you to do.

With regret, Irsei turned toward the southeast. Her heart ached at all the lives lost. She would surely be hunted now. There would be no place she could hide now.

I promise you, once I am finished with this realm, no one will even dare go near you. Worry not of these meaningless pawns. They all want to kill each other, anyway. You are simply quickening the pace and giving them what they want.

Irsei ignored her. She just wanted to get back to her cliff and rest. She would be glad when this was all over, and she could disappear to a new realm.

I find it amusing that you believe I will release you soon.

The words froze Irsei in mid-air. "You said you would when you were finished with Sacia!"

Oh, my poor naïve little pet. Why would I ever give up such a powerful tool? I might need you again someday. Oh, and don't go trying to kill yourself again either. I will never allow you to do such a thing, but I will make you wish you were dead if you try.

Irsei let the words soak in for a few moments and hung her head. Somehow, some way, she would break the spell this witch had on her. This was not something she thought of, as she knew the witch could read her mind. This was something she knew to be truly deep in her soul.

Chapter Forty-Five

As both armies approached, King Rhys and King Cameron both halted their armies, stepped forward, but stopped several yards apart. Rhys sat quietly on his horse and measured his adversary. Cameron scowled at the Elven king and spat on the ground.

"King Rhys, you and your… people… occupy our ancient lands. Surrender now and I promise to make your deaths a quick one. If you choose war, your deaths will be slow and extremely painful."

Rhys sat quietly for a few extra moments to annoy Cameron more than anything. He calmly looked over at his commander.

Paro rode up beside his king, and Rhys looked over at him. "What do you think of this deal, commander?"

Cameron cast an evil grin. "Can the king not make his own decision? He must call on someone beneath him to answer?" He laughed and the whole Sacian army joined in, laughing hysterically with their king.

Rhys ignored Cameron, and Paro simply shook his head.

"I don't believe I care for it much at all, my king. I've grown accustomed to living on our lands. I formally suggest we keep Paelea and fight to live."

Rhys nodded to Paro. "I agree with you, commander." He then turned to Cameron.

"While I appreciate your more than gracious offer of killing us quickly over the alternative, I believe we will decide our own fates. You may return to Sacia at your convenience."

Cameron growled. "Slow torture it is. Enough talking. It is time to cleanse your filth from our lands."

"You're welcome to try. You fight for dominance while we fight for survival. We'll see who comes out the victor."

Commander Girout watched the Elven lines and noticed Liam in front. He whispered to Cameron and pointed to where Liam stood. Scowling, Cameron glared at the Paelean king.

"I see the former Prince of Sacia has turned traitor. I'm not surprised. He's as much of a coward as his father was. They will celebrate his death as much as yours, Rhys."

Cameron addressed his army. "Liam survived and became a traitor. He fights against his own people and cannot be trusted. Ignore any propaganda he spills, because I assure you, they are all lies."

Liam looked at Rhys and the Elven king nodded, giving Liam permission to speak.

"Fellow Sacians! I fled my homeland because my uncle betrayed my father and me. I survived his assassination attempt on my life and fled to avoid any more attempts against me!"

The Sacian army murmured amongst themselves, but Cameron waved to them to be quiet.

"These are all lies that he speaks. I have reports he colluded with the elf to kill his own father to take the crown for himself! The proof is right in front of you! He stands with our enemy! Is this the king you want? Or do you wish to have a king who will place Sacia first?"

The soldiers cursed Liam and chanted, "KING CAMERON! KING CAMERON!"

They repeated it over and over, and chanted so loud they drowned out any rebuttal Liam had. Liam slumped on his horse and tried once more to plead for them to listen. It was no use. Cameron had them riled to a frenzy. There would be no reasoning with his people. He fell back into formation. There would be war yet again.

Both kings and their entourage turned back to their respective positions and readied for attack. Horns blared from both sides and while the Sacians cheered and mocked their enemy, the Paeleans stood stoically, watching the Sacians closely. Commander Girout raised his sword, yelled the command to charge, and pointed his sword toward their enemy.

The armies of Sacia and Paelea clashed fiercely as the two lines met. Archers from both sides rained arrows down amongst the soldiers, thinning the ranks only slightly. Liam led a smaller group that included Evan and Theron, while Rhys and Paro led the others with the main bulk of soldiers. Liam's aim was to target Cameron. If he could capture or kill him, that might stop the battle before too many men from either side were killed. Liam's group fought their way through their fellow countrymen as they pushed their way deeper through the front. The Elven soldiers who accompanied them were some of King Rhys's elite warriors and helped clear their way to where Cameron was positioned. Elite infantry and cavalry surrounded him as he barked orders to his surrounding soldiers.

Evan looked briefly at Liam. "Sure wish we had Raven and her crazy sister with us right now. That witch alone might have made this a little easier."

"I'm not so sure Raven's even alive," Liam replied. "What she did was suicide."

Evan shrugged. "As if you're one to speak."

"Yeah, that was not one of my finer moments."

"You two should court. You're both alike."

Liam glared at his friend. He opened his mouth to say something when a sword came to his face. He ducked, parried, and drove his sword into the assailant. Liam ignored Evan's last statement.

"I'm sure she's fine. She's been quite resourceful."

"Let's pray you're right, old friend!"

*****

Cameron, oblivious to the threat heading his way, continued shouting commands at his army. Liam took notice that his group was taking losses as they ventured deep into the Sacian army. While their first wave of attackers were mere boys or men that lacked much training, they were venturing into more elite soldiers now, some he even recognized.

He nodded to one off to his side, but he just sneered back, yelling obscenities at Liam. He just sighed and pushed on.

*****

A Paelean soldier approached Paro. "Commander! Riders are approaching! They appear to be Paelean!"

Paro moved away from the battle and watched them close in the distance. Rhys followed and stopped beside his commander.

Rhys stared ahead. "If it is, it's not good news."

The riders met up with them. "My king! My king! The castle was attacked!"

"Attacked? By whom?"

"We thought at first it was Sacia. As we made our way behind them, we glimpsed their armor and they looked more Sleston than Sacia."

"Sleston?"

Rhys bristled. "Commander Paro! We must retreat to Paelea! The castle is under attack!"

Paro started to relay the order when he saw a speck up in the sky coming toward them. As it came closer, Paro realized what it was. "Dragon! To the forest! Everyone, NOW!"

Rhys repeated the plea, and the Paelean army scrambled for the forest. They sounded their horns to reach those out of earshot. From there, Paro would lead them back to Paelea. Soldiers still engaged in battle were caught dead center in the dragon's path. Liam was out there somewhere. Paro said a silent prayer for them and fled for cover.

*****

As they were but a stone's throw from Cameron, Liam heard horns blaring behind him. He took a glance back but could see nothing but the carnage of battle. Liam stole a look up and saw something dark in the distance. It looked like it was coming toward them. He looked back and found Cameron locking eyes with him. Cameron ordered soldiers to attack.

As they prepared for the onslaught, the small group heard shouts and cheering behind them.

Evan shouted at Liam. "What's going on?"

"I don't know. I heard what sounded like Paelean horns."

"You are correct, prince." One of the Paelean soldiers replied. "Those are calls to retreat. I fear all is lost."

Theron looked up and Liam saw him turn white.

"Theron, what is it?"

"It can't be!"

Liam looked back up and yelled for everyone to fight their way toward the forest.

"Is that a dragon?" Evan asked, unbelieving.

Liam stared in astonishment. "That's what it looks like! Let's go! Now!"

Chapter Forty-Six

Irsei probably should have circled around to attack the fleeing Paeleans but felt she did what she needed to please the witch. She made one more pass at the Sacian army, thinning the ranks even more as they fled in terror to anywhere they could hide. The dragon then flew back up into the clouds to finish the witch's request and burn Sacia. Perhaps then, she might return to her home, even if to wait for the next horrible deed to be commanded by her.

*****

Lisabet sat her food down and closed her eyes. For several moments, she sat motionless. Irsei was now on her way to Sacia. Soon, Lisabet knew she would need to leave so she could make herself known to what was left of the human kingdom. Raven snapped her fingers repeatedly in front of her mother's eyes, trying to bring her out of whatever trance she was in. She finally opened her eyes and was startled, seeing Raven so close. Lisabet quickly waved her right hand and Raven went flying across the room and crumpled against a wall. Lisabet sat back while Elysia jumped up to check on her sister.

"I'm so sorry, my child. I must have blanked out for a second. You startled me!"

Raven groaned as Elysia helped her to her feet. Raven rubbed the back of her head and winced in pain.

"What happened?"

"It must be a residual effect from being in that trance for so long."

"Yeah, that must be it," Raven said with disbelief. With the aid of her sister, she walked back to where her dinner was and sat down. No longer hungry, she just grabbed her cup and poured some ale she found within the cave. *Not bad*, she thought.

"Dinner is delicious, Raven! Where did you learn to cook like this?"

"Years of being on my own and not wanting to starve, I guess." Raven didn't even look up at her.

"You haven't found a man yet to cook for?"

"No, I don't need any baggage in my life."

"What of your sister? Is she baggage as well?"

"I keep trying to get rid of her, but somehow we keep bumping into each other."

Elysia laughed. "You're so funny, Raven."

"Yeah, I'm hilarious. Anyway mother, what are you going to do now that you're free from this… spell?"

"Oh, I just have a few loose ends to tie up before I can find a new start. Would either of you want to assist me in this quest?"

"Of course, mother!" Elysia said immediately.

Raven put her hand on her sister's arm. "What do you mean by quest?"

"I will not sit by while the people who did this just go free. I want justice for what happened."

"The people who did this are gone."

"So, you believe their families who praised them for it should go unpunished then?"

"Their families, at this point, are innocent. They had absolutely nothing to do with those you accuse."

Lisabet watched Raven for a moment and tapped her finger to her chin. She turned to Elysia, who was watching them go back and forth.

"Sleep now, child."

Lisabet raised her hand and placed a spell on Elysia. She yawned and laid down on the floor and closed her eyes. Lisabet then turned to Raven with a more intense glare.

"I can see you do not believe me, Raven." Lisabet walked up to her without breaking her stare.

"I don't. You are hiding something, and I demand to know what."

Lisabet's eyes flared.

"Demand?" She laughed devilishly. "You think you can demand anything of me? Your mother?"

"You might be my mother, but you are no longer my mom. You've acted strange from the moment you 'awoke' from this so-called spell."

"How dare you speak to me like this! You may have discovered your magic, but they are weak compared to mine. I will have vengeance on what happened to me, and I will not allow, even you, daughter, to stop me. YOU, of all people, should understand me!"

Raven nearly buckled at her mother's glare but held firm. "If being a bounty hunter has taught me anything, it is that vengeance will only get you hurt or killed. It also won't erase the wrong that happened to you. No one of importance now had anything to do with what happened. You must see that."

"Maybe not, but people will always fear what I might do. Look at your sister. She's been hiding her whole life because of her magic. Is that the future you want for yourself as well?"

"You think killing people will stop them from being afraid of you?"

"I *want* them to be afraid. I want them to see me and fear what I am."

"Where will this end, mother?"

"That's simple. I'll start with Sacia and once I have conquered them, that will force Paelea to submit to me. One by one, nations will bow to me until I am empress of this realm."

"Empress? You sure think highly of yourself. I assume with you telling me this, you plan to kill me."

"Oh no, dear Raven. I would never kill my own daughter. Your sister will do it."

At that moment, Lisabet turned toward Elysia and ordered her to rise. Raven backed up a step and switched her gaze from her mother to Elysia.

"I command you, Elysia, to kill this woman standing before you. She is not your sister, but an imposter."

Raven backed up some more. "Elysia, that's not true and you know it."

Elysia turned and stared at Raven. Her eyes changed from purple to white. Raven saw a single tear fall from her right eye and knew Lisabet had full control over her. Elysia rotated her hands and created a violet sphere between them. Her expression turned to anger as she pushed the sphere toward Raven. She tried to dodge, but it struck her in the side. Raven slumped to the ground as purple lightning surrounded her body and attacked her nerves. She screamed in pain as Elysia shoved another sphere toward her. Raven glimpsed her mother as she smiled. Her own mother was enjoying watching one daughter kill the other. Anger filled her mind. Lisabet walked behind Elysia and rubbed her hands through her hair.

"Do not stop until she's dead, Elysia. Once you are done, return to your home and I will summon you to where I'll be when I need you. Do you understand me?"

"Yes, mother. This imposter must not interrupt our plans."

"Good girl." She turned to Raven. "At least I have one daughter I can count on."

Lisabet, confident Elysia would finish her sister, walked out of the old fortress and to the edge of the cliff. She spread her arms and as she stepped off, transformed into a falcon, and soared away. Her revenge was going exactly as planned.

Chapter Forty-Seven

The Paelean army raced through the forest toward their homeland. King Rhys thought of not only the possibility his daughter was dead, but of his people as well.

A dragon? Here? I thought they had all vanquished a century ago. Now one shows up as we fight once again with the Sacians. There must be something darker at play here.

Rhys tried to block the negativity from his mind and focused on getting to his castle. The Sacian army scattered and appeared in worse shape than they were. He doubted any would continue to pursue them. They would probably scramble back to their homeland to see if the dragon was headed there.

Soon, up ahead, the forest thinned, and he knew his kingdom was near. As they finally left the forest, Rhys could see smoke rising over the castle walls. His fear turned to anger, and he pushed ahead of the army and raced as hard as his horse could go. He slowed as he approached the smoldering entrance. Dead bodies from both sides lay all around, and he spotted a couple of guards who were checking bodies to see who might still be alive. They spotted their king and immediately kneeled.

"Don't. Please. Rise and continue your search. My daughter… is she… alive?"

"Yes, Princess Amedee lives. She is in the shelter, along with others."

King Rhys rushed past them and made his way toward the shelter. Liam, Evan, and Theron were not far behind. Before he entered, he turned around and confronted the three men.

"See if these guards need help. There might be others who are still alive."

"We will." Liam said. "Let us know if you need anything."

Rhys nodded and then entered the shelter and found Amedee on a makeshift bed. She turned and saw her father rushing to her and smiled.

"Father do not worry. I am healing up fine. Portia's taking good care of us."

One guard spoke up. "Portia's a witch, my king! She's using magic!"

Rhys looked at Amedee, who shot a stern look at the guard.

"She's helping the wounded, including me! Witch or not, she is one of us!"

The king looked proudly at his daughter and laid a hand on the guard's shoulder.

"Magic or no magic, she appears to be helping everyone. Portia is my daughter's closest aide and if she trusts her, so do I."

"Yes, my king. My apologies."

"It's been a trying day and everyone's on edge."

Amedee gave her father a worried look. "What do you mean? Did you not win the battle?"

"I'm not sure anyone did. A dragon attacked as we were fully engaged with Sacia. I believe they suffered the most. We saw the dragon in time and had a better chance of evading it."

"The dragon?" Amedee began trembling. "It was here as well."

"So, the Slestons didn't cause this damage?"

Amedee shook her head. "No father. We fought them to a near standstill. We wouldn't have survived another charge, however, as our gates were weakening. As much damage as the dragon caused, I think it inadvertently saved us as well. The Slestons were all but annihilated, and those who survived disappeared into the forest."

"I fear we may have been spared for now, but I can't shake this feeling that with a dragon reappearing, something darker will follow."

Chapter Forty-Eight

Elysia stared at her sister like she didn't know her at all. Her eyes remained white, and she looked at Raven as though she were looking through her and not at her.

"I don't know what you did with my sister, but I will kill you for it."

Raven winced in pain as the energy coursed through her veins. "I AM your sister, Elysia. Mother has spelled you to not recognize me!"

"No, you are an imposter who killed my sister. Now I will return the favor."

Raven's anger continued to build, and she felt the fire within her building. Elysia must have sensed it as well, hitting Raven with more energy.

"She… is… using you… Elysia. Can't you… feel her in… your mind?"

"I feel peace knowing mother is going to end this war and I won't need to hide any longer."

"She's…" Raven forced the rest to come out. "Lying to you!"

"YOU'RE the liar! You killed my sister! Now, just DIE!"

Raven screamed and felt herself burning. She could no longer feel the energy pulsating from her sister. She felt rage erupting from within and the pain that came with it. Raven began to spasm until all at once, fire exploded from her body in a ring around her and caught Elysia right in the chest. The force of the wave blew Elysia off her feet and slammed her into a nearby wall. She crumpled to the ground, unconscious. Raven raised her head up long enough to see her sister lying motionless before she collapsed from exhaustion.

*****

Raven awoke hours later with a splitting headache. She dragged herself to her knees and scanned the room. Lying against the wall was her sister, with blood splattered around her. Raven forced herself to stand up, wobbled over, and slumped down beside Elysia. She checked for a pulse and found it, but it was weak. She thought about tying her up in case she was still under their mother's spell, but she was too weak to do it. Raven let destiny decide her fate. She concentrated on what little strength she had to ignite a small flame in her hand. She stared at it for a few moments, still finding it hard to believe that she possessed magic. Raven watched the flame flickering in her hand for a moment longer.

"I don't know about you, sis, but I've no strength to fight you anymore today. Hopefully, you're back to your crazy old self. Here goes nothing."

Raven moved her hand to Elysia's arm and let the flame touch her sister's skin. Elysia groaned and then let out a small whimper.

She opened her eyes and looked up at her sister. Raven noticed her eyes were no longer white but that annoying purple she had grown to appreciate.

"Wh-what happened?" Elysia groaned.

"Our mother happened. She's been mind-controlling you since before we started this journey. I don't suppose you have some type of protection spell to keep her out of your head, do you?"

"I know one that should work for now. Help me to my feet and I will do one for both of us. We must be quick, though, before she realizes we're awake. This will only last for so long, but it will give me time to make a couple of talismans for us."

Raven reached out her hand and pulled her sister to her feet. Elysia propped herself against the wall and gathered herself for a moment and chanted. She waved her hands in front of her, and a white orb appeared in front of her and split in two. One engulfed Raven as the other orb did the same to Elysia. The magic absorbed into both of them, and Raven could feel it take effect.

"Are you sure this will work?" Raven asked.

"Yes. As powerful as our mother is, she won't be able to break through this spell."

Elysia looked around her and then stared at Raven for a moment.

"Did I really try to kill you?"

"Yes, you did, and I owe you one for that. In fact, this entire journey has been me against you and mother."

"I'm so sorry, Raven. I never meant to hurt you."

"I know that, but ever since we met, I feel like my whole life has been spiraling out of control. I've been tortured, almost killed multiple times, and now I'm up here on a mountain away from everything and we just released a powerful witch upon the world. I'm a little tired of it."

"Soooo… then do something about it."

Raven squinted her eyes at her. "What?"

"Stop being the victim, Raven. With this protection spell, I see clearly again for the first time since I asked you to come with me. I know what mother is now. You think I'm crazy and maybe I am. Being alone for so long, hidden from the world, has made me mad to an extent, I guess. What I'm trying to say is let's go after her. She might be powerful, but together, we are equally powerful."

"I barely even know how to use my magic and when I do, I'm too exhausted to do anything after."

"That's because you try to use it all at once. There is a time and place for that, but a little magic can go a long way, especially if you learn to control it. I am much more in control of my magic than you are, yet you stopped me."

"Well, dying brings that out of me, I guess."

Elysia looked down at the ground. "I won't ever forgive myself for that."

"Nonsense. You never saw it coming. I didn't know she was even alive, much less turned into an evil witch."

"I should have, though. I sensed your magic when you didn't even know you had any. I… I should have known."

"Enough. We've got to warn King Rhys about mother. I know she's going after Sacia, but she said she wants to control the entire realm. Do you feel up to traveling now?"

"I'll do a couple of healing spells before I make the talismans. We are going to need every advantage we can get if we are going to go after mother."

"Good. As soon as you're ready, we'll leave."

Chapter Forty-Nine

King Cameron rose from some rock outcroppings and watched in disbelief as the dragon flew toward Sacia. It came from the direction of Paelea, but it couldn't have been the elves who sent it. It killed a good portion of their army as well. *Why now?* Cameron thought. Why now when Sacia was so close to victory?

Commander Girout cleared his throat to get the king's attention. Cameron snapped out of his thoughts and turned his attention to his commander.

"We should return to Sacia to see if the dragon attacked the castle."

Cameron watched as the Paeleans retreated through the woods and turned his attention to what was left of his army. Too many men were lost to even hope to chase the Paeleans at this point. He only hoped the Slestons had better luck.

"Yes, commander. I think we should return to Sacia." Cameron took one last look at his enemy and sighed. "Sound the retreat. Let's go home."

*****

Liam looked out from a southern watchtower and surveyed the landscape. So much had happened in such a short time it made his head spin. Betrayal, murder, magic and now dragons. Had something triggered all of this or was it built up over time and he just missed the signs? In his defense, he had cared more for bard women, ale, and sparring with Evan to care about anything else. He should have seen the coup coming, but he was caught up in his own nonsense. Here he was now in another kingdom and a refuge from his own people who wanted him dead.

Liam thought over and over of ways to rid Sacia of Cameron and one word kept springing up in his mind: Raven. Was she truly dead?

What about Elysia? He wondered if she might be back at her home, grieving over her lost sister. Liam decided that was what he must do. Evan, of course, would want to go, as would Theron. Liam felt they would be better served here. He needed to attract as little attention as possible so he could sneak away and do this alone. Evan and Theron were currently busy helping with the wounded. Now was the perfect opportunity to slip away. He knew he would draw the ire of King Rhys, but he needed to find out what happened to Raven. If he could find her and convince Elysia to join them, they might bring Cameron down together.

Convincing the guards at the front gate that he was simply going to take a quick look outside, he casually made his way along the base of the outside wall. As he approached the nearby forest, Liam took a quick look up at the nearest watchtower. Luckily it was empty, so he took off running and once he made it deep into a thickly wooded area, he glanced back and found no one following him. Sword at his side, he gripped the handle once for reassurance and then started his journey to find Raven.

*****

Evan emerged from the Safehouse to get some fresh air. He looked around and saw no sign of Liam. Curiously, he asked the guards at the gate if they had seen him. They mentioned he went to check around outside but hadn't returned.

"Dammit!" Evan swore aloud. "I should have known not to leave him alone for this long!" He addressed the guards again. "Did you see where he went?"

"Sorry, we did not. He's been gone for a while, though."

Evan shook his head. He had to tell the king of this.

What are you doing, Liam? Are you trying to get yourself killed?

Chapter Fifty

Queen Brayla was sparring with one of her nobles when her top advisor approached. She held up her hand to stop the match.

"Aiken, this certainly cannot be good news if you are interrupting me."

"No, your Majesty. I'm afraid I bring grave news. A couple of our soldiers returned from Paelea."

Aiken paused a moment before continuing.

"They're afraid most of our soldiers are lost."

Queen Brayla raised an eyebrow.

"Lost? What do you mean by lost?"

"They claim Paelea was besieged. They had set up camp to plan their next move."

"Is this going to take all day?" Brayla said impatiently.

"They, um, claim a dragon came from the north."

"A dragon? Is this some sort of trick?"

"No, your Majesty. The dragon attacked both armies. Our men became trapped in the prairie below the castle walls. They never stood a chance. Some made it to the forest, but most perished from the dragon's fire."

The queen stood speechless for several moments.

"We offered some of our best trained warriors with the promise they would receive little resistance. Cameron said nothing of dragons! Where are the men now?"

"With our medics receiving treatment."

"Take me to them, now!"

"Yes, your highness."

Brayla dismissed her nobles and followed Aiken to where the men were recovering. She looked at the caregivers and waved a hand at them.

"Leave us, now."

The three ladies bowed their heads and scurried from the room. Brayla turned her attention to the two soldiers. She folded her arms and peered at them.

"Tell me what you know."

The men told their queen how they had spotted something in the sky coming toward them from the north. They explained how they had the castle besieged and had set up camp for the evening. By the time they realized what the object was, it was too late. The camp scattered in every direction, and they had barely made it to the woods. Everything around them was ablaze, so they kept running deeper into the forest until they felt they were safe. At that point, they felt they needed to notify her of the situation, and they barely slept or eaten until they returned.

Brayla listened intently to their reports and frowned.

"You just ran and left your fellow soldiers behind? You didn't go back once this supposed dragon left?"

The men looked nervously at each other. "W-we just thought you should know as soon as possible."

"No, you ran to save your own skin. If this… dragon, as you call it, wanted to attack us here, we would have already been attacked long before you made it back."

"B-but…"

"Silence! I will decide your fates later, but for now, a night in the dungeon should give you both some time to think."

They both bowed but kept their heads down.

Brayla called the women back in and told them to finish tending to them. As she left, she told the guards to take them to the dungeon for the night, but to treat them civilly. Outside the healing facility, Lord Aiken approached and walked beside her.

"Did they truly see a dragon, milady?" Aiken asked.

"I don't know, but they seem convinced. If this is true, I'm not sure what this means. What I know is with Sacia and Paelea resuming their hostilities, Sacia might be ripe for the taking. Even if we lost most of the men we sent to Paelea, we still have a formidable force to deal with a war-torn Sacian army. I think we should plan an attack on Sacia, and the sooner, the better. Whether or not Cameron knew of this dragon, he is bloodthirsty, and it will only be a matter of time before he sets his sights on us."

Pass this along to Sir Tedric, so he will begin preparing. I will update when I think we should attack.

Aiken bowed. "Yes, your highness." Brayla nodded at him, and he turned and headed toward Sir Tedric's quarters.

Chapter Fifty-One

Raven and Elysia began their descent down the mountain. The storm that ravaged before was gone, but the wind was still howling. They could hardly see through the blowing snow, and their faces stung from the bitter cold. Elysia leaned into Raven. "Where are we going again?"

"Paelea. We need to warn King Rhys. It might be too late, but we have to try."

Elysia shook her head. "That might not be a good idea, seeing how we are the ones who released her."

Raven shrugged. "We might leave that part out for now. It's going to be hard to stop our mother if we're executed."

"A valid point, sister."

After several moments of silence, Raven nudged Elysia. "I don't suppose you can just snap your fingers and whisk us off to Paelea, huh?"

Elysia laughed. "I can do short jumps at a time. If it's the two of us, it really drains my power. It might take us longer to get there, as I would have to stop to rest more often. I would need time to recharge. Besides, I need to have already been to a place in order to go there. I've been practicing this more, but it really takes a toll. I need to become more in tune with my magic."

Raven looked back at her. "You seem pretty strong to me."

"Yet you overtook me fairly easily when I was throwing all of my magic at you."

"Desperation can have that effect. If I hadn't knocked you out, you would have killed me."

Elysia frowned, but Raven shook her head.

"I'm not bringing that up to guilt you, just as an observation. I was lucky, is all."

The women stayed silent for the rest of their descent. As the land flattened out before them, the wind slowed to a light breeze. The air was warmer, thankfully. Elysia reached out to feel the sun on her hands and closed her eyes.

"It's hard to imagine anything horrific happening by looking around. Everything is so serene now."

"Yeah, it's a shame evil is so prevalent in these lands. If not for our mother and Cameron…"

Elysia interrupted. "There would be others to take their places. I don't believe our mother to be outright evil. I just think she's been wronged so many times that her judgment has been manipulated."

"Manipulated? By whom?" Raven asked incredulously.

Elysia shrugged. "By her life experiences. She's been hunted, betrayed, and almost killed. To her, the world has failed her, and she seeks to correct that."

Raven glared at her sister. "She's not back in your head, is she?"

"Not at all. Just looking at things from her perspective is all. Just like you possess her anger. Yours is more forward though, while hers is more calculated."

"Take that back, Elysia! Don't you dare compare me to that witch!"

Elysia rolled her eyes. "Forgive me. I don't know where I would have come up with that."

Raven kept her glare on Elysia for a moment longer. The sting of what she said caused her to snap, but almost immediately, she saw the truth in her statement. That didn't stop her from pointing a finger at Elysia. "I am nothing like our mother. I would never try to destroy an entire realm for vengeance."

Almost immediately, they both heard someone or something coming. They were nearing the forest that stretched all the way to Paelea and while the forest was still an hour away, the brush was thickening before them. Before they had time to hide, a figure stumbled from behind one of the bushes, and fell at their feet. A soldier with a makeshift crutch from a limb looked up at them and begged them for water. They saw fear in his eyes, and they looked down and saw blood still oozing from his right leg.

Elysia bent down and gave him a drink while Raven asked who he was. He didn't look like he was from Sacia or Paelea. After taking several huge gulps of water, he mentioned he was from Sleston. His voice cracked as he kept talking over and over about a dragon attacking.

Raven told him to be quiet for a moment.

"I just have a couple of questions for you. Why is Sleston even here? Your lands are northwest of here."

"We were helping King Cameron against Paelea."

The soldier reached for her water pouch, but she pulled it from his reach.

"We had them surrounded, but they summoned the dragon!"

"A dragon, you say?"

"Y-yes! I thought they were extinct, but… but it wiped us out… or most of us, anyway."

Raven looked back at Elysia, but she just shrugged her shoulders.

"I am no friend of Sleston, but you look as if you have suffered enough." Raven handed him the pouch, and he guzzled.

"I assure you, there is no dragon here. Rest up and then return quickly to Sleston. I don't want to come back and see you here or my witch friend here will turn you into a toad, understand?"

The soldier looked worriedly at Elysia, who formed a purple orb in her hands.

"Yes, ma'am! I will leave within the hour! Thank you for your kindness."

Raven simply nodded and turned to her sister. Elysia had extinguished her orb and linked her sister's arm in hers, and grinned.

"You didn't kill him and even showed him, dare I say, some kindness!"

Raven shook loose from her and glared.

"One more smartass comment from you and I'll go back and kill him with my bare hands."

"Sure, you will, you old softy. So… a dragon, huh? You don't seem surprised by this."

Raven gave her a sarcastic stare. "Well, let's see. I met you and not only are you a witch…" Elysia bristled at that word, and Raven rolled her eyes. "Okay, sorceress." Elysia grinned. "Anyway, not only that, but you are also my sister. I discovered I have magic as well and that our mother is alive and an evil maniac. So why not dragons? Magic was extinct, yet here we are." Raven brought up a fireball in her hand and stared at it for a moment and extinguished it.

"You're a quick learner," Elysia observed.

"Yeah, let's hope I learn faster. We need to hurry now and see what might be left of Paelea."

Chapter Fifty-Two

Evan found the king sitting by his daughter.

"Your highness, I need to speak with you about Liam."

King Rhys knew from the look on his face this wasn't good. "Go on."

"Liam went outside the walls and hasn't returned."

"I see. Do you think they captured him?"

"No, I know Liam as if he was my brother. I think he took off to find Cameron. I fear he might try to do something reckless and get himself killed."

"What do you ask of me?"

"I know you cannot spare any soldiers to look for him. I was wondering if I could request Erinoth's help."

"You wish to take Erinoth to track Liam?"

"Basically, yes. Unfortunately, I wouldn't be able to pay him anything now. Once this war is over, I promise to pay him handsomely."

King Rhys thought for a moment. "You are correct that I cannot risk any of my soldiers to search for him, but I will allow Erinoth to go with you if he so chooses. Because of what he has faced with the Sacians, I won't order him to go."

Evan bowed. "I understand, your highness. Liam means well, but sometimes, he jumps before he sees what's below."

The king looked at his daughter. "I know all too well what you mean."

"Father!" Amedee, who had been silent this whole time, gave her father a stern look.

King Rhys smiled and then turned back to Evan. "Go, with my blessing. Liam is a determined fighter. Whatever he has in mind, he should not have gone alone. That's suicide."

"Thank you, your Majesty." Evan bowed once more and turned away to look for Erinoth.

"You want *me* to go look for Liam with you?" Erinoth asked quizzically.

Evan nodded to the elf. "You're a scout. Isn't that what you do?"

"Yes, I'm a scout, but you're not. I know how to sneak around without being noticed. You, not so much."

"Trust me, being Liam's bodyguard is like being a scout. He's always tried to slip away from me, and I've always found him."

"So why not just go then? Why do you need me?"

"Because I need to find him quickly. I don't know what he's up to, but if something happens, I will never forgive myself. I promised King Warrick I would always look after him."

Evan paused for a moment. "I heard what happened to you and Raven at the castle. I know you don't trust Sacians for good reason. However, Liam is not Cameron. Liam is the rightful ruler of Sacia and a good man. He wants only to put an end to this decades old war, and he will do it on your king's terms. I am sworn to protect Liam not only for his title, but because we are lifelong friends. I will swear that same oath to you, Erinoth."

"I am not only a scout for King Rhys, but I am also his ears within the kingdom. I watched you as I was skeptical of three Sacians showing up to fight against their own people. I've seen the sacrifices you've made for the Elven people and why you are doing it. I want peace as well and it is because of this why I will help you, Evan. Give me a little time and I will meet you at the front gate."

"Thank you, Erinoth." The elf nodded at Evan and turned and exited. Time was slipping away, and Liam was only putting more distance between them. Evan hoped his friend knew what he was doing this time.

Evan was waiting at the gate when he saw Erinoth approaching. "Well, let's get going. The sooner we find Liam, the sooner you can get back here. Thank you again for coming."

"No need to thank me. Liam is an honorable man and if something happens to him, Cameron will be the legitimate king, and that does not bode well for Paelea. So, by helping you, I am helping my people."

"Fair enough."

The pair walked to the edge of the forest, and Erinoth shook his head. "With all the activity in these woods the last couple of days, it will be hard to track him. Do you have any idea where he might be headed?"

Evan thought for a minute. "I don't think he would head straight for the castle. That would be suicide and he knows it. The only place I can think of is where that crazy witch lives. He could be looking for either her, Raven, or both."

"Well, that gives us a place to start. Do you remember where she lives?"

"Vaguely. I think if we get close enough, I should remember from there. I know it's not too far from the castle, but it is well hidden."

Erinoth nodded. "We'll find the prince. Hopefully, before he does something foolish."

"Yeah," Evan agreed. "He's known for that."

*****

Raven and Elysia arrived at Paelea to find the elves recovering from the Sleston attack. As they neared the still smoldering gate, two Paelean guards stepped through, swords drawn.

"State your business!" warned a guard.

Elysia smiled at them. "You dare threaten a couple of damsels in distress?"

Raven shook her head at her sister. "We need to speak to King Rhys immediately. There is a threat looming bigger than any war with Sacia."

"Yeah, well, we already know about the dragon, so you best be on your way."

"Wait, a dragon did this?" Raven asked.

"Most of it, anyway," the other guard replied.

"The dragon is only part of the problem. I urge you to allow me to speak with your king now. This is an urgent matter not only for Paelea but for the entire realm."

"We don't have time for this. The palace is closed to outsiders, so you need to leave… now."

Raven started to say something, but she noticed her sister's eyes glow.

"My sister asked you nicely to take us to your king." Elysia waved a hand in counterclockwise motions. "I'm telling you to take us to him now."

The guards stared at her for a moment and lowered their swords. "Follow us."

Raven looked over at her sister, and Elysia winked back at her.

"Are you just going to stand here and stare, or are you going to follow these nice men?"

Raven rolled her eyes, and they caught up to the guards, who were already halfway across the courtyard. They led the sisters to a hidden shelter. The guards stepped inside, followed by Elysia. Raven closed the door behind her and scanned the area. She saw all the wounded lying throughout the shelter. She felt the rage build in her. Her mother had done this. She had somehow compelled the dragon to attack the Paeleans. Her sister must have sensed her anger as she laid a hand on her arm. Raven looked at Elysia, who simply shook her head. She was right. Raven knew she had to control her temper, especially here. Elysia pointed to where King Rhys was sitting by a bed. Was that Amedee he was sitting by? Raven made her way over to the Elven king.

King Rhys looked over and saw Raven and Elysia coming his way. So, Raven survived after all. He nodded to them as they approached. They bowed, and both looked at Amedee.

"Is she okay?" Raven asked nervously.

"She is now. She was badly injured from the dragon attack, but Portia has been healing her."

Elysia perked up. "How?"

"Magic apparently. I didn't even know she was…"

"A witch?" Elysia cut in, folding her arms.

"Elysia!" Raven glared at her sister.

Rhys waved a hand at her. "It's okay, Raven. We have laws against such practices, but there hasn't been magic in these lands in decades. There are those who frown upon magic users for fear of the unknown. However, Portia's shown she means no harm and has my daughter's trust, so I'm willing to overlook it."

"Will the citizens have an issue with it?" Raven asked.

Rhys shifted so he could face the sisters directly.

"They can come and share their grievances with me if they wish, but I'll simply remind them of everyone she saved today. Out of curiosity, why are you two here?"

Raven explained to the king about their journey north and about their mother.

"We have reason to believe she's behind this dragon attack."

Rhys's eyes widened. "This is troubling news indeed. What is your mother's name?"

"Lisabet."

Rhys thought for a moment and abruptly stood up.

"Lisabet? Lisabet's your mother?"

Raven lowered her head. "Yes, your highness. I'm still trying to wrap my head around it myself."

"I heard the stories about her from my father, but I thought she was dead."

Raven paused for a moment. The king had been welcoming to her and her sister, but she didn't think he was ready to hear the truth about how Lisabet was released.

"She's not, I'm afraid. She revealed herself and tried to recruit us to help her. We declined, but as you can see by my face, she didn't take rejection very well."

"You both were fortunate to survive if she's as powerful as the stories say."

"I don't think she's given up on us yet. However, she doesn't know how stubborn I can be."

"What about you, Elysia? Will you be able to resist her again?"

Elysia had been quiet up to this point. She looked at her sister and then at the Elven king. She dropped her gaze to the ground and answered.

"I-I'm pretty sure I can."

"Pretty sure?"

"I'm certain I can, your highness. I did once already."

King Rhys glanced over at Elysia and then raised an eyebrow at Raven.

"Why do I feel I'm not being told the entire story?"

"I was a child when I was told our mother died. I must have repressed a lot of memories because I don't remember my mother being pregnant. To be honest, I remember little at all from that time period except my mother's death. Elysia was told our mother died when she was born. So, we were both lied to and kept separated all these years. My sister was ecstatic that our mother was still alive, while I was quite skeptical. She wanted us to come together as a family and right whatever wrongs she believed had happened to her. We refused, and she began torturing me with her magic. Elysia intervened and helped me get away from her. At that point, Lisabet said she wasn't through with us. She said she had something important to take care of first but would find us in time. After she left, Elysia did a couple of healing spells on us and then we came straight here."

Rhys sat quietly for a moment. He glanced down at his daughter and wondered how any person could treat their own children in such a way.

"Thank you for this information, Raven. I'm not sure where we go from here, but I'd rather know another variable is involved than being blindsided again. As you can see, we are limited in what we may offer you. There is some bread and ale over in the far corner. Let them know I sent you over."

"You are too kind, King Rhys."

"Both of you have proven to be friends with Paelea. In these times, friends are a rare treasure."

Raven and Elysia bowed and made their way to the table in the corner. When they asked the men in charge of the rations, they looked toward the king, and Rhys nodded back at them. They found a spot along a wall and sat down. Raven surveyed the room and was taken aback by all the wounded. She watched with sadness as a body covered with a blanket was carried out. This was the work of her mother. She wished at this moment she had learned of her magic years ago. She was in a dangerous phase in that she still couldn't completely control her powers. Lisabet was a much more powerful witch. Raven and Elysia both were handled easily by her, and Elysia was compelled to kill her own sister.

As they finished their bread and ale in silence, an aide to the king approached. He told them the king wanted a word with them. The sisters looked at each other and followed the man over to Rhys.

Raven bowed. "You wished to speak to us, your Majesty?"

"I failed to mention before, Liam left looking for both of you."

"He did? How long ago was this?" Raven asked.

"It's been three days since he left. Evan and Erinoth left to track him."

Elysia linked her arm with Raven's. "I think we might find him a little quicker if we may take our leave."

"Of course, Elysia. Stay safe. Keep me updated if you find anything more about your mother's plans."

Raven nodded. "Of course." She looked at a sleeping Amedee and gently laid a hand on her shoulder. "Rest well, princess. We have much to discuss when you are better."

The sisters bowed to the king once more and left. Once they passed through the makeshift gate put up while they were inside, Raven turned and looked at her sister. "How are we going to find Liam before Erinoth? He's an expert tracker."

Elysia smiled. "Yes, but I'm a well-rested witch!" She winked at Raven at calling herself a witch and Raven simply rolled her eyes. "I'm willing to bet he is heading to my house to see if we're there and we will be. Grab my hand."

Raven clutched her hand tight and Elysia laughed. "Not so hard, silly. We're not exactly flying." Before Raven could interject, Elysia encircled them in a purple haze and the two sisters disappeared.

Chapter Fifty-Three

The two women reappeared at Elysia's house. As they approached the front door, a falcon swooped down and materialized into their mother, Lisabet.

"That's quite a powerful protection spell you have, Elysia. Unless…" Lisabet eyed the matching talismans on ropes around their necks. "I have underestimated you. Talismans, that's smart. However, when I could no longer sense either of you, I went back to the cave and followed you all the way to Paelea. I heard everything. There's no need to continue searching for your Liam. He's inside and not in very good shape, I'm afraid."

"Enough!" Raven sneered at her mother. "Let Liam go."

"I don't think I will, daughter. You know how much I love my playthings."

"Yes, we saw what your dragon did." Elysia responded. "Let him go. Keep him out of this."

"Oh, my naïve daughters. He is very much a part of this. He is heir to a throne that will be no more. Now, throw me your talismans or I will kill him now."

"How do we know you even have him?" Raven shot back. "This may be nothing more than a trick."

"It is no trick." Lisabet flicked her wrist and the front door opened. Liam came floating out, gasping for breath and his toes dragging in the dirt.

"Now, I won't ask again. The talismans, now."

Elysia and Raven looked at each other, and Elysia nodded. They both took them off at the same time and tossed them to the ground in front of Lisabet.

Raven glared at her mother. "There, we did as you asked. Let him go."

"Of course." She waved her hand and flung Liam into a tree, and he collapsed to the ground. Elysia ran to check on him. She nodded back to Raven.

Raven ignited her hand and shot a quick fireball at her mother, blinding her momentarily. "Elysia, disappear with Liam, now! Don't tell me where. Just go!"

"But Raven!"

"No buts! Now, quickly!"

Elysia nodded with a tear in her eye and grabbed Liam and disappeared as Lisabet reached for her magic. Raven lunged and took her mother to the ground. Hand held high, she conjured another fireball and, as she released it, Lisabet used her magic and shoved her off of her. Raven went flying and landed several yards away with a thud. She groaned as she tried to stand up but was shoved to the ground and felt herself pinned. Her rage built, and she felt her body heating when Lisabet simply shook her head, muttered a few words she didn't understand, and watched the world around her fade to black.

*****

Raven awoke and found herself back in the cave she and Elysia found their mother in. She tried to raise herself up but found she couldn't move. Raven was on the bed her mother was in when they saw her for the first time. She could move her eyes and saw Lisabet approach her.

"Irony, don't you think? You wake up where I was, and I am on this side with my skepticism. Don't bother responding because you can't. In fact, in a few minutes, you won't even know who you are. My body is still weak from being here for so long, so I am going to borrow your body for a while. Maybe even permanently. Who knows?"

Raven looked at her in horror as Lisabet began chanting. She didn't understand the language she was speaking, but she felt herself getting weaker. Almost as if her body was leaving her. She had to fight this. Somehow, she had to hide herself away in a corner of her mind. Her mother was taking over her somehow, but she had to hold on. She saw her mother lie down out of her vision. Raven retreated her soul to the far reaches of her brain and locked herself inside. She could no longer feel her body and knew her mother had completely taken over.

"I can still sense you, daughter. No matter. You will continue to weaken until you are no more. I will keep my other body hidden here in case I need it again. Let's see what chaos we can cause with the woman known as Raven."

For the first time since she didn't know when, Raven was truly frightened. Her own mother was killing her daughter's soul. For vengeance for something done years ago. Her own mother. She had to hold on, for Elysia's sake, and for Liam. Raven didn't know how, but she would break her mother's hold on her. She had no other choice except to die.

Epilogue

Elysia reappeared with Liam and they both fell at the edge of a lake. At the same lakeshore she had found Raven. Right outside of the Sacian kingdom. She brought an injured Liam almost right to Cameron's doorstep. Elysia cursed herself, but she hadn't had time to envision a place to go. Somehow, her subconscious had brought them here. With her magic severely weakened, she tried dragging Liam toward the forest. She could barely move him a few inches. With her last remaining strength, she lifted Liam with her depleted magic and got just inside the cover of the forest when she collapsed on top of him. She had heard guards nearby, but she was sure they hadn't heard them. She realized as she was blacking out that Sacia was burning.

*****

Lisabet played with the long red locks of hair from her new body. She felt more alive than she had in years. Oh, to be young again! She immediately sought Irsei, and the dragon explained her destruction of the Sacian castle.

Excellent, Irsei! You have done well, my pet. I am finished with you for now, so go rest until I summon you again.

Lisabet stared into the mirror at a nearby table and smiled. "Such a waste of a beautiful woman, Raven. You should have had several children by now."

Lisabet paused for a moment. "I don't know how it's possible, but I still can't sense your sister. No matter. She can't hide from me forever. We have work to finish. In the meantime, I am going to visit this Cameron of Sacia. He's going to be surprised to see me... I mean you. Raven. I doubt you are going to be as pleasurable, or as wild with your magic as last time."

Lisabet walked out of the cave and stood at the edge of the cliff and felt the wind blow through her hair. Hands held out wide, she leaped from the edge and transformed back into a falcon and set her sights toward Sacia.

About the Author

(Photo courtesy of Jim Fort, Addison Photography)

Anthony D. Butler is originally from south Alabama but has been an Idaho resident for over twenty years. While most of his jobs centered on the tech fields, his passion has always been to become an author. The general idea for *The Raven Chronicles: Magic Reborn* had been floating around for years, but it wasn't until 2017 that Anthony created a story from this idea. A year later, he put pen to paper, and by 2021, he completed a full manuscript.

Anthony, when not writing, enjoys exploring the diverse landscape Idaho offers. Between the various mountain ranges, the lush grasses of the Camas Prairie, and the desert landscape of Southern Idaho, there is plenty here to draw inspiration for his writing.

Magic Reborn is only the beginning, as he has several books planned to make this an ongoing series.